PRETEND IT'S LOVE

A BEHIND THE BAR STORY

STEFANIE LONDON

Entangled Publishing, LLC
2614 South Timberline Road
Suite 109
Fort Collins, CO 80525
Visit our website at www.entangledpublishing.com.

Lovestruck is an imprint of Entangled Publishing, LLC.

Edited by Alycia Tornetta
Cover design by Heather Howland
Cover art from Shutterstock

Manufactured in the United States of America

First Edition September 2015

To anyone who's ever chased a dream against the advice of others.

Chapter One

There were plenty of other things Paul Chapman would rather be doing than watching two people make goo-goo eyes at each other. He could stab himself in the eye with a steak knife. Or listen to his mother talk ad nauseam about the intricacies of the floral arrangements.

Either would be preferable.

"Man, you've got to lighten up." Noah Reid, his best friend and soon to be fellow groomsman, elbowed him in the ribs. "You look like you're about to go all *Friday the Thirteenth*."

"I hate pretentious parties." He shoved a bite-size piece of toast with smoked salmon into his mouth. "And I hate this stupid, tiny food."

"What did you expect?"

Noah had a point. Paul should have known what he was in for the second his brother announced the engagement party would be held in his fiancée's family home in Toorak, aka the "old money" part of Melbourne. The Greenes were rolling in it. It was fitting that they'd be drinking the fanciest champagne on the market and eating food that looked fit for a dollhouse.

"Is it so bad that I want a burger and a beer?"

Noah laughed. "If you're still hungry we'll do a Macca's run on the way home."

"Deal."

Paul watched the happy couple. His big brother looked more satisfied than he'd ever seen him, and Gracie, his pint-size wife-to-be, wore a smile that managed to out-sparkle her impressive engagement ring.

"Reckon that will be us one day?" Noah asked, studying Des and Gracie as though they were an alien species.

"No way. Marriage is for chumps." Paul screwed up his nose. "I'm only here because of Des."

Stomach grumbling, his eyes roamed, already on the hunt for something else to eat. The current options were miniscule sushi rolls and pieces of raw fish. What was the point of eating something if you weren't going to bother cooking it first?

He brought a champagne flute to his lips and knocked back the remainder of his drink. It wasn't his poison of choice but it *was* alcoholic. Better than nothing.

A gloomy funk had descended over Paul ever since the engagement had been announced. He was happy for his brother, of course. Gracie was good for him and they'd worked hard to get past the early hurdles in their relationship. But it was just another opportunity for Des to prove to their family that he was the favorite. The golden child. The chosen one.

The son who would live up to all their expectations.

Des ran the restaurant and bar, First, where Paul worked. His big brother's success in business would be further complemented by a wedding. Then it wouldn't be long before the bambini arrived, and Paul would never have a hope of catching him.

A waiter walked past carrying a tray of freshly filled champagne flutes. Paul switched his empty glass for a full one and downed half of it in a single gulp.

"Whoa there. You're drinking like an eighteen-year-old girl at O week." Noah shook his head, laughing. "I don't want to be holding your hair back later tonight when that all comes back up."

Paul opened his mouth to retort, but Des and Gracie were coming their way. He put on his best "happy brother" face and held his champagne flute up in salute. Gracie launched herself at the two guys, collecting them both in a hug that was impressive for a girl her size.

"How are my future brothers-in-law?" she asked.

Noah might not have been a flesh and blood brother, but the Chapman boys—and now Gracie—treated him as if he were part of the family.

"Enjoying the festivities. Paul here has taken a liking to the champagne." Noah smiled innocently as Des rolled his eyes.

"Me, too." Gracie leaned forward and winked at him, her cheeks flushed.

"Too many drinks, not enough dinner," Des said with a frown. "We should get something into your stomach."

"Don't be a bore. I haven't drunk like this since university—it's a special night!"

"Can I get that in writing so when you're glued to the bed all day tomorrow I can remind you the hangover is worth it?"

She poked her tongue out at him before turning to Paul. "Was he always this straight-laced growing up?"

"Uh, yes," Paul replied. "Hard to believe it, but he was worse."

"Yikes." Gracie giggled, covering her mouth with one hand.

When she wandered off to dance with her sister, Des shook his head. "The wedding planning has been a little... tense."

Noah frowned. "Because of Mrs. Greene?"

No one ever referred to Gracie's mother as anything but Mrs. Greene, although Paul had been led to suspect her name might be Cecilia. Despite sharing her daughter's petite stature and flair for style, she lacked any of the warmth and charisma that Gracie exuded, and had a reputation as being a bit of a dragon.

"Yeah." Des raked a hand through his dark hair. "She's driving Gracie bananas, but I can't get involved. She gets worked up if I mention it. Good thing it'll be over in a few weeks."

Paul choked on his drink. "A few weeks?"

"Yeah, we're going to announce it tonight. The wedding is going to be in six weeks."

"Is she..." Noah looked around to see if anyone else was in earshot.

Des folded his arms across his chest. "She's *not* pregnant."

"Not yet," Noah said, waggling his eyebrows.

"Why the hurry?" Paul set the champagne flute down.

Des looked over his shoulder. "I don't want this planning

phase to go on any longer than it has to. Besides, we're ready to be married. It sounds corny, but I don't want to wait any longer."

Paul made a gagging motion. "What chick flick did you pull that from?"

"Mock me, oh little brother. One day this will be you, and I'll be the first one to remind you of this moment." Des turned to Noah and slapped him on the back. "And when it comes to the wedding you have to wear a suit. No excuses."

Noah had worn black jeans and an open-collared shirt under a leather motorcycle jacket, despite the fact that the invites had said *Dress Code: Cocktail.* "It'll be the first time."

Des moved on to talk to Gracie's older sister and left the two men to their drinks. The engagement party was intimate. Private. Immediate family and the bridal party only.

But the wedding would be filled with people Paul didn't want to face. Most of all, his ex-almost-fiancée and the guy she'd married…who just so happened to be his cousin.

"Six weeks, can you believe it?" Noah shook his head. "How are we going to plan a buck's party in that time?"

"Yeah…"

But Paul's mind was consumed with the wedding itself. He'd thought that Gracie and Des would have a more standard engagement, like one or two years…five, if he was lucky. Then he would have time to get his shit sorted, find someone he trusted enough to bring to a family function, and do something noteworthy so he didn't have to rehash the overdone conversation about his lack of direction in life. He could hear his aunts now.

Paul, why can't you be more like your brother? Why haven't you settled down with anyone yet? Don't you want to get married?

And the underlying question beneath it all: *what did you do that was so bad your girlfriend cheated on you with your own cousin?*

Like it was his bloody fault.

"Hey." Noah waved a hand in front of his face. "I said, do you think Des would want a weekend away for his buck's?"

"Maybe." Paul wanted to talk about *anything* that wasn't connected to the wedding, but his concentration had deserted him.

"You giving a speech?" Noah asked.

Paul looked up. "Huh?"

His friend pointed to a piece of paper sticking out of his suit pants pocket. "I thought you hated speeches."

"I'm not giving a speech, but I did get her number." He nodded toward the blond catering assistant who flushed when the two men turned to look at her.

"This is a family event." Noah shook his head.

Paul grinned. "Girls love me, what can I say?"

"You're so full of shit."

Truth was he hadn't really wanted her number, but old habits die hard. At one point women were the center of Paul's life, though not any one woman in particular. However, lately he'd stopped going out partying with Noah. He'd even deleted all the numbers in his phone that weren't family or his mates. Empty encounters had begun to fill him with resentment.

The kind that burrowed deep down and made you question everything.

The sudden decline in socializing hadn't gone unnoticed; both Des and Noah had questioned him to no avail.

He didn't want meaningless sex anymore nor did he want to be chained up in a relationship hell. If only he could have some kind of in-between solution…

But now Paul had bigger problems to deal with other than his sex-life limbo. Tonight's announcement meant he had only six weeks to find someone to stand by his side at the wedding *and* do something meaningful with his life. No big deal, right?

There was no way in hell he'd front up to his ex alone being exactly the same guy as when she'd dumped him two years ago. Not going to happen.

Libby Harris begged her cell phone not to ring again. After four calls bearing bad news, she was about ready to hurl the damn thing out a window. This couldn't be happening.

One press release and her business—which was on the brink of launching—was going down the drain faster than a Britney Spears comeback. Maybe if she stopped answering her phone the bad news would disappear.

"Stay calm." Her best friend, Nina Bauer, sat cross-legged on the couch in Libby's office and mimicked deep breathing. "I know it seems bad, but there's room in the market for more than one person. Everything will be fine, and we'll probably laugh at this in a few months."

"Laugh?" Libby held up her iPad with both hands and thrust it in Nina's general direction. "My business is going to die because I didn't launch early enough. That's nothing to laugh about."

"Freaking out *isn't* going to help the situation." Nina pushed off the couch and grabbed the iPad, gently setting it down on the coffee table. "And stop waving your gadgets in my face."

One month out from her launch party, Libby's business—a line of girlie infused vodkas and cocktail mixes—was in peril. That morning a press statement had been released that the infamous reality TV star turned sex-tape celebrity, Kandy K, was launching her very own line of flavored vodkas.

What were the friggin' odds?

Now all the businesses she'd lined up to stock Libby Gal Cocktails were dropping like flies—they wanted to jump on the celebrity bandwagon. Despite her social pedigree, Libby Harris was *not* a celebrity.

"We don't know how many places are going to pull out. Maybe the worst of it is over."

Libby dropped her face into her hands and tried not to hyperventilate. "I'm going to fail because I never made a sex tape. How ironic is that?"

Her phone rang again, and Libby threw it into the drawer of her desk, slamming it shut with a resounding bang. She couldn't take hearing one more restaurant owner tell her that they were "very sorry" but they needed to put their business first and "explore other options."

They didn't even have the guts to admit *why* they were dropping her.

"Trust me, in a few years you'll be happy you don't have a sex tape." Nina pulled open the desk drawer and retrieved the phone. "There's no point sticking your head in the sand. We need to focus on fixing this problem. How many are we down to?"

"Six, I think." Libby flipped open her laptop, scanning down the details neatly typed into a spreadsheet. "I had ten restaurants lined up for the soft launch in Melbourne; four have pulled out so far. But I'm pretty sure that"—she pointed at her phone, not daring to pick the damn thing up. It may as well have been a venomous snake baring its fangs—"was Lulu Bar."

"So we go into damage control. Let's meet with the restaurant owners and see what we can do. Don't they say market competition is good?"

Libby balled her fists. "This is not good, it's a bloody disaster!"

Nina sighed and grabbed one of the bottles of Libby Gal Cocktails infused vodka that sat in an open box, awaiting shipment. "Marshmallow and rose petal, my favorite. Just what the doctor ordered."

She screwed the top off before Libby could protest and fished out two of the branded shot glasses that were supposed to go along with the order. The sight of her business logo—a martini glass with a lip print on the side and her initials in pink and green—made her suck in a breath.

"We shouldn't be drinking the stock, Neens."

"Heavy drinking is often recommended in times of intense stress." Nina winked and waved the bottle in front of Libby's face.

Libby laughed despite herself. This was *exactly* the reason she was friends with Nina. The woman could put a smile on her face no matter how dire life seemed.

"I'm pretty sure that's the opposite of what's recommended."

Nina shrugged and set the shot glasses on Libby's desk, free pouring until the liquid reached the edge of the glass. "Bottoms up."

Libby brought it carefully to her lips. She downed the drink in a single gulp, shutting her eyes and letting the alcohol work its magic. The sweet scent of marshmallow and rose petals danced in her nose. It was the first flavor she'd ever made.

The business had started out as a hobby when she'd infused store-bought vodkas in pretty jars and given them as gifts for Christmas and birthdays. When Nina got married she asked Libby to make her a special blend for wedding guest gifts. Compliments and requests came rolling in, and Libby put her medical degree on hold to turn her passion into a business.

It was the first time she'd ever taken a risk on herself.

"Hit me again." Libby slammed the glass down on her desk and gritted her teeth.

She would *not* let her business die. She would not admit defeat because of bad timing. And she most definitely would not crawl back to her father and tell him that he was right.

"That's my girl." Nina grinned and blew a strand of her electric blue hair out of her face as she refilled the glasses. "Cheers."

Libby tipped back the second drink and dropped down into her desk chair, surveying her office. The room was originally a spare bedroom, but she'd turned it into her own personal command center. Boxes of product were piled up in one corner, and her adorable vintage couch and coffee table were covered in Nina's artwork for the launch party. Her desk was a bit of a hot mess, but she still had her beautiful makeshift flower vases—some of the prototype Libby Gal Cocktails bottles—holding rainbow bouquets of roses and oriental lilies.

This was her dream, and she would fight for all of it. Kicking off her towering emerald-green stilettos, she turned her laptop to face her. Slowly, she ran one pink lacquered nail down the column of restaurant contacts and jotted down names and addresses on a notepad.

"What are you going to do about The Chief?" Nina jumped onto the desk, swinging her bare feet back and forth. "You know he's going to be all over this like a rash."

Though her father was a world renowned surgeon, he approached everything from parenting to washing his car with a style more suited to the military. Hence the nickname.

"I'm hoping that he'll be too wrapped up in his latest wife to have noticed," Libby said.

"You think he won't mention it? Yeah right." Nina twirled a strand of her blue hair and let out a sigh. "He'll latch onto *anything* right now if it means dragging you back to his life plan."

"I guess I'll have to cross that bridge when I come to it." Libby pursed her lips. "But I know one thing for sure, I'm not going back to med school."

Chapter Two

Libby gritted her teeth and strode along the footpath, ignoring the throbbing pain from a nasty blister on her heel. She'd been on her feet all day, dashing from one meeting to another in shoes that were better suited to a stilt walker than a burgeoning entrepreneur.

But her look was part of her brand—bright hair, big heels, in-your-face lipstick. People noticed her because of the way she looked, then she made sure they remembered her for what she said. She wasn't giving that up, blister or no blister.

Sadly, nothing had helped her today. She was zero for ten…every single business she'd signed for her launch had backed out. If her life was a game then she'd hit the biggest damn snake on the board.

Her phone vibrated in her hand, but she didn't bother to check who was calling. Her father had been trying to get a hold of her for three days, ever since the press release that ruined her business had hit the papers. She hadn't even bothered to listen to his numerous voicemails, because she knew *exactly* what they would say. Her father was circling, sensing a chink in her plan—an opening, a weak point, a precious sliver of vulnerability.

After all, daughter dearest had deviated from her path, and he'd been hating every minute of it.

Libby laughed to herself, it was the only response that wouldn't encourage the onslaught of tears. She'd done right by him her whole life, she'd tried to be the daughter he always wanted. The perfect Grade A student, the Mini-Me to his Dr. Evil. And now that she finally wanted to do something for herself, was he happy?

Hell no.

Still, at least *he* called. That was more than she could say for her mother.

She shoved the still-buzzing device into her handbag and kept walking. Eventually she'd need to take his call, but after an abysmal day of rejection she needed a drink. Normally getting home to work on a new cocktail or test out a new infusion idea would be priority. But not today.

The buzzing started up again, and Libby rummaged around in her bag to find her phone. She wouldn't give her father the satisfaction of answering his call, but she *could* turn the damn thing off so she didn't go insane. She continued walking as she hunted for her phone, her blood pressure rising with each step. Maybe she should answer his call if only so she could tell him what an arrogant, selfish, mean—"Hey!"

Libby looked up at the sound of the warning but her shoe connected hard with a solid mass. Pain ricocheted through her ankle as the world tilted beneath her feet. A strong hand wrapped around her arm, wrenching her back to standing just as the sound of glass shattering pierced the air around her.

It took her a moment to realize her eyes were squeezed shut, although against what she wasn't sure. Pain and mortification were neck and neck.

Libby cracked an eyelid open, her breath catching in her throat. The man holding her wore a tight black T-shirt that amply showed off solid arms and broad shoulders. But it was his face that made her chest squeeze and her mouth run dry. The fading daylight cast shadows across him, highlighting razor-sharp cheekbones and full lips. His eyes—edging on black—were covered with heavy lashes, and his hair had been cut short, though it didn't hide its natural kink.

He held a now-empty tray in the hand that wasn't wrapped around her arm. Libby risked a glance at the floor and cringed.

"Are you okay?" he asked, his dark brows narrowed in a way that made her unsure whether he was concerned or furious. Maybe it was a little of both.

Her brain grappled for a response, but the fireworks going off in her body were more than a little distracting. It seemed that if you spent long enough away from the opposite sex that first "re-introduction" would wreak havoc on one's hormones.

"I'm fine." Libby mustered a smile; she was not the sort of girl who got flustered by a hot guy...usually. Now embarrassing failures of coordination on the other hand... "Uhh... thanks?"

"Was that a question?" He released her slowly, his dark

eyes tracking her movement.

She tried to put pressure on her foot but fiery pain shot up her leg, making her gasp. "No."

"You're not okay." He put the drinks tray down on the table. The bar's name, First, was artfully carved into the wood in funky, tattoo-style font.

For some reason the name sounded familiar.

"Neither are your glasses," she said miserably looking down to the glittering shards decorating the footpath. "Did I get them all?"

"Every single one." A smile twitched at the corner of his lips. "But glasses can be replaced. That ankle looks like it needs some TLC, though."

"I'm fine." She tried to stand normally while keeping all her weight on her good foot.

Stupid weak ankles and stupid, *stupid* heels. This day could not get any worse.

His face told her he wasn't buying it. "Let me help you inside. You can take a seat, and we'll call you a cab."

Did she have to embarrass herself in front of the hottest guy on earth? No scratch that, guys like him weren't best described as hot. Striking, perhaps…or exciting. Darkly sensual.

She swallowed. What happened to being a confident, intelligent, and powerful woman? That was the Libby Gal Cocktails brand. Her signature. But today every ounce of confidence she owned had slinked off with its tail between its legs, and now she was playing damsel in distress. Ugh.

"You look like you could use a drink anyway." He smiled, holding out a hand to her. "I make a mean Negroni."

"Can you make it in a vat?"

"That bad, huh?"

She hesitated for a second and then took his hand, a shiver running through her at the slide of his palm against hers. The grip was sure, strong…yet gentle. He abandoned the drinks tray and came closer to her, tugging her arm around his shoulders and supporting her weight against him. They moved slowly, and each step made their bodies press together.

Libby clamped her lips together to keep from crying out as the pain in her ankle worsened.

The bar looked warm and inviting. Golden light spilled through the open door, and the calming sounds of chatter and jazz music beckoned.

"How you holding up?" His easy smile and dark eyes made her heart thump as they stepped into the restaurant.

"Apart from the mortification," she muttered, "I'll be fine once I get that drink."

There were a few steps down from the doorway to the main area, and she could already feel her ankle protesting.

"Are you going to be able to get down the steps?" he asked.

She hesitated and a second later he'd scooped her up into his arms and was carrying her down the steps and across to the bar.

"You can put me down now," she protested, covering her face with the hand that wasn't clinging desperately to him.

She hated heights, and he had to be at least six one… which would mean a painful landing if he dropped her. But he walked with her in his arms as though he was only carrying a bag of sugar. Confident, in control.

He probably thought she was a hot mess.

"Do you normally rescue clumsy girls in the street?" she asked as he stopped at the bar and set her down gently on a barstool.

"I'm a bartender; clumsy girls are my specialty." He flashed her a smile as he reached over the bar and grabbed a pile of folded dishtowels. Placing them on the stool opposite her, he dragged it closer so she could rest her foot there. "You need to keep this elevated. I'll grab you something cold to put on it."

"You're a regular first aid specialist," she quipped as he came back with a bag of frozen peas.

"Our barista has a habit of burning himself, so we always keep these handy." He placed the peas on her ankle and removed her shoe.

Each brush of his fingers against her bare skin made her stomach flutter. Talk about a real Cinderella moment.

"There," he said, standing back and admiring his work. "Now how about that drink?"

"Thank you." She chanced a look at him, and the dark stare sent shockwaves through her.

Oh yeah, this guy had lady-killer written all over him.

"So you've had a rough day?" he asked, heading behind the bar.

She sighed and checked out her surroundings. "The roughest."

The bar was actually a bar and restaurant, the intimate tables obscured from the street's view. Being a Tuesday night the room wasn't especially packed, but they'd filled enough tables to take home a respectable amount, she suspected. The other barstools were empty, except for a lone beer drinker at one end.

"What'll it be?"

How about you? Naked. Now.

"I'll take you up on that Negroni. It's been a while since I've had one." Libby dug her hand into the bag on her lap, hoping to hell he couldn't read her mind. She pulled out her phone and saw the four missed calls from her father. Ignoring them all, she texted Nina with a pleading request to come and pick her up.

"Now that's a crying shame. I don't get to make them too often, a lot of the ladies who come here either drink wine or vodka sodas." He screwed up his nose and grabbed an orange from a container below the bar. "Pretty boring."

"I'm definitely more of a cocktail girl."

"Music to my ears." He looked up, flashing her a brilliant smile that just about had her panties dissolving.

He deftly sliced the orange so a chunk of peel curled away from the flesh. Gin, Campari, and vermouth were added to a glass filled with ice and stirred. Then he ran the peel around the edges of the glass, squeezing it before dropping it into the sunset-colored drink.

Between his bartending skills and the way he'd carried her, Libby could tell this man was good with his hands…*very* good. A tingle ran the length of her spine, stirring her in all the right places.

"That looks delicious," she said, hoping to hell he didn't realize that she was referring to him and not the drink.

"It's on the house." He placed the glass in front of her. "On one condition."

She sipped the drink and let out a small sigh as the perfect flavor danced on her tongue. An artful medley of sweet and bitter. "Which is?"

"You tell me why your day was so crappy…you know, other than crashing into me and breaking all my glasses."

She flushed. "I'm working on a business venture, and it's not going as well as I would like," she said, fighting her natural desire to put on a confident face and sweep the bad bits under a rug.

He leaned forward, bracing his hands against the bar. "What's the business?"

"I sell infused vodkas and cocktail mixes." She took a sip of her drink. "Well, I was going to before all the places I'd lined up pulled out at the last minute."

"No wonder you were walking like you had a train to catch."

"I put my studies on hold to start up this business." The words came tumbling out as though this gorgeous bartender had pulled out an invisible cork. "If I can't make it work then I'll have to go back to university. My father's doing everything in his power to manipulate me into giving up…"

"Ah, family." He laughed, the sound hollow. "They always complicate things."

Libby nodded, looking down into her already half-empty glass. Warmth spread through her, loosening her limbs and her tongue, dulling the throbbing in her ankle. The Negroni was a serious cocktail and could do a lot of damage on an empty stomach.

But getting drunk seemed like an excellent idea right about now.

"How come you decided to be a bartender?" She took another swig of her drink.

"All the jobs for rocket scientists were taken," he joked.

"I don't know. It chose me as a career... I'm good with alcohol."

"Drinking or mixing?"

"Both." He chuckled, raking his hand through his hair and offering her a devilish smile. "Although I'd say slightly better at drinking."

"Cheers to that," she said, picking up her glass and draining the rest of the cocktail. "How about another?"

"That problem is still going to be there tomorrow." He accepted the empty glass from her and commenced making another cocktail.

"Can't a girl have one evening of denial?" She dropped her chin into her hands and sighed.

Flattening his palms against the bar, he leaned forward. "Why did all the restaurants decide to pull out?"

Swallowing—and trying not to stare at how perfectly defined the muscles in his arms were—she considered her options. There was no harm in telling him the real reason, as horrible as it would be to repeat.

"Do you know who Kandy K is?"

He shook his head.

"She was on that reality dating show where they stick everyone on a remote property and they have to fend for themselves and they all end up sleeping with one another by the third episode?"

He looked at her as though she'd sprouted antennae and had started speaking an alien language. "Uh, no."

"Anyway, it's D-grade TV. She was on that show and then someone leaked a sex tape of her and some football player—"

"Ah, yeah." He snapped his fingers. "And now she hosts

some late night radio talk show."

"Yes, that's her."

"What the hell does she have to do with your business?"

"Well." She sucked in a deep breath. "Kandy K is bringing out a line of infused vodkas, and all the restaurants I had lined up to launch my product are now backing out for a chance to get her stuff instead."

"Right." He frowned and raked a hand through his hair.

"Since she's partnering with one of the big vodka companies the exposure is going to be huge." Libby stared at her empty glass, willing it to refill itself. "There's no way they'd take a chance on some one-woman band when they could have that instead. It's so frustrating working your butt off for something and then have it completely crumble right in front of you."

He wouldn't know... When had Paul ever *really* worked for anything? He breezed through life on charm and charisma, at least that's what his ex had said.

The girl in front of him looked up with her huge eyes. They weren't brown, but they weren't green, either. At this close distance he could see the flecks of gold and gray that speckled her irises, the half-moon of green that sliced through the honey-colored rings.

They were like her—intriguing, unusual, and sexy as hell.

She was a whirlwind of energy. It had certainly felt like a tornado struck him when she'd smacked into him at full speed, knocking the glasses straight off his tray and stealing the breath right out of his lungs. Not to mention he'd had to keep control over his body's natural reactions when he'd picked her up and felt the brush of her sweet curves against him.

She wasn't even his usual type. He was a die-hard blonde man and this girl's hair was like the color of a copper coin. Most of the time, he found himself attracted to the life-of-the-party type, the girls who were the ones dancing even when there was no dance floor. She looked like she knew how to have fun, but there was a serious streak to her. She was sharp, intelligent.

Different.

"You have to at least tell me your name," he said, running another curl of orange peel around the edge of her glass and dropping it into the drink. "In case this evening of denial ends up with me needing to call someone to pick you up."

"Guess," she said with a smirk, reaching out and taking the drink from him.

"You want me to guess your name?"

"Yeah." Her rosy lips wrapped around the edge of the glass as she sipped. "What kind of girl do I look like?"

"One who knows how to lead a guy straight into trouble."

He folded his arms across his chest, resisting her bait. Lips quirked into a smile, she waited for him to answer her question, her eyes locked onto his in silent challenge. For a moment the rest of the restaurant faded away; the ambient sounds dissolved into nothingness as his whole world focused in on her. For some reason the little staring contest made his blood pump harder, his competitive side stirred by the tilt in her chin.

"If you don't guess then I won't tell you my name," she

threatened, smiling.

"I'll have to call you Tiger then."

"Tiger?" She threw her head back and burst out laughing. "Why on earth would you call me Tiger?"

"We had a cat called Tiger growing up. He was ginger and his fur was exactly the same color as your hair."

"Great, so you're telling me that I remind you of an old cat." She tried to sound offended, but her eyes sparkled and amusement bubbled in her voice. "That's charming."

"I'm calling it. Bartender one, Tiger zero."

"My name is Libby." She extended her hand over the bar. "Don't call me Tiger."

"Paul."

A zing of electricity rocketed through him as her small palm slotted into his. Her skin was smooth and creamy, but she had a handshake as firm as any guy he'd ever met. It was the kind of handshake that warned him not to underestimate her.

"So this isn't your bar?" she asked, releasing his hand.

"Nope." He busied himself with wiping down the countertop. "My brother runs this place."

One of the waiters came past and handed over an order slip. Two boutique beers and a house G&T. Boring.

"It looks like he's doing well for himself," Libby said, sipping her drink.

Paul bent down to the fridge below the bar and pulled out two beer bottles. He popped off the caps and set them down on a tray. "We got a write up in Gastronomy Magazine recently. They called us one of Melbourne's up and comers."

"Really?" Libby raised a brow and nodded her head. "That's quite an honor. I'm surprised you could squeeze me in tonight. My grand entrance notwithstanding."

"Week nights are still a little slow," he replied with a smile. "But we're packed on Fridays and over the weekends now. We had a queue right around the corner last Saturday."

The article had been a huge win for First and reservations were up all around. They'd had to hire two new waitresses to keep up with the demand. Paul felt a surge of pride run through him, despite the fact that it wasn't a win for him personally. But he wanted First to succeed. His brother deserved it.

"Hey, man. Don't tell me you've resorted to hitting on girls who can't run away." Noah appeared at the bar and winked at Libby. "I left some paperwork in the back office. Have you got the key?"

"I'm perfectly comfortable here, thank you very much." Libby said primly, sipping her drink.

"If he's hassling you, just call out." Noah came around the bar and dug his elbow into Paul's ribs. "Although we never seem to get any complaints, do we? The ladies love him."

"What the fuck?" Paul muttered under his breath, glaring at his so-called friend as he dug the keys out of his pocket.

"Relax, she knows I'm joking." Noah grabbed the keys from Paul's hand. "Gee, can't take a little friendly ribbing tonight, can we? This is payback for always stealing the pretty girls in high school. That was uncool, and you know it."

"That was years ago." Paul turned to Noah so Libby couldn't see his face. "Are you going to hold that against me forever?"

As Noah sauntered off, Paul turned and caught Libby

watching him closely, her hazel eyes sweeping over him in unconcealed analysis. What did he care if she believed that he was a shameless womanizer? It's not like he'd see her again.

But the very thought made his stomach turn.

"It's amazing how one little article can make such a big difference," she said, graciously turning the conversation back to the bar. "You know, this is *exactly* the kind of place that would be perfect for my cocktails."

Topping the gin off with tonic water, Paul grabbed a slice of lime from the dish in front of him and wedged it onto the glass's rim. He signaled to the waiter to come and collect the order.

Libby looked at him expectantly. There was something about her sincere face and those beautiful, intoxicating eyes that made him want to help her. He knew little about her business and nothing about her personally, but she stirred in him some basal desire to protect.

"You should talk to my brother." He hunted around for the business cards that Des had recently ordered but couldn't find them.

"That would be great."

He grabbed a napkin and a pen. "Here's his name and number. He'll be in tomorrow morning."

She plucked the napkin from his hand and finished the rest of her drink before fishing around in her bag and pulling out a lipstick and mirror. A woman with blue hair came up to the bar and placed a hand on Libby's shoulder, her face creased with concern.

"Looks like the cavalry is here," Libby said.

Light glinted off the gold casing on the lipstick as she

dragged the color across her lush, full lips, her mouth opened into a small *O* shape.

Lipstick was high up on his list of things he wished girls wouldn't bother with—it got everywhere, and it tasted gross. But watching Libby apply it was the most erotic thing he'd seen in a long time. The way the color made her lips look full and moist caused all the blood in his body to rush south.

There is something seriously wrong with you. Lipsticks should not give you a hard-on.

Chapter Three

The following week Paul sat in his mother's kitchen, bracing himself for their weekly "chat"—if you could call it that. Did guilt mongering count as conversation?

"You're not getting any younger you know."

"I'm twenty-seven," Paul said, shaking his head. "You act like my whole life is over."

"I already had your brother and you by twenty-seven. I was married *five* years." His mother's Italian accent had softened over the years, but it always came back full strength when she engaged guilt mode. "My parents brought us to Australia so we could make a better life."

"And I'm disrespecting that because I'm not married and reproducing?" He leaned back in the rickety dining chair, wishing for the hundredth time that his mother would replace the yellow plastic set and bring her kitchen into the twenty-first century. She sat across from him, still wearing the floral apron from when she'd cooked lunch. "Des is only just getting married."

"Your brother is responsible," she said, reaching for the carafe of water between them and refilling their glasses. "I knew he would settle down, but he was concentrating on work. You…"

"What?"

"You have a new girl every week; it's not right." She shook her head, the reading glasses lodged in her curly, dark hair sliding precariously. "Don't think I'm stupid, Paolo. I know. You can't keep changing women like you change…shoes."

Every Friday he had lunch with his mother before his long shift at First. And every Friday she grilled him about why he wasn't in a relationship, why he mooched off his brother, why he wasn't doing anything with himself.

Apparently that now also included criticizing his dating choices.

"Seriously?"

"You think life is all fun and games."

For a moment she looked sad, the lines around her eyes deepening as she frowned. That look killed him every damn time. Guilt sliced through him, and he hated himself for not being what she wanted…not that he would *ever* let her know that. On the outside he looked as stubborn as ever, but her words tore at him. Shredding him up little by little.

This was a preview of things to come at Des's wedding. Sadie. His cousin. His aunts. A reminder that he'd disappointed everyone by not being…someone else.

"She's pregnant, you know," his mother said, interrupting his thoughts.

"Gracie?"

"No."

His heart stopped for a moment. "Who?"

"Sadie." She sighed. "Zia Marcella rang today, Sadie is sixteen weeks pregnant."

The air rushed out of his lungs as though someone had punched him in the stomach. The thought of seeing her at the wedding was bad enough, but knowing she was pregnant...

"I have to go." He pushed up from his chair and grabbed his leather jacket from the coat stand.

"Paolo." She stood, crossing her arms under her bosom. "I don't say these things to upset you."

He gritted his teeth, fighting the pounding in his head. He needed to sort out this problem soon. He was not going to face his ex and her smarmy husband alone while they basked in the glow of their perfect life.

The life he had wanted.

"I'm not upset, Ma." He shrugged into his coat and swallowed against the lump in his chest. "I've got to get to work."

"I want you to have a good life." She looked up, her black-brown eyes shining.

"I'm perfectly happy with my life."

At one point he was sure that was true, but now he constantly battled restlessness and dissatisfaction. Pride wouldn't allow him to let anyone else see that, though, and he wore his reputation as armor. Better to be a womanizing playboy—as his mother had once called him—than to be a loser.

He *had* to come up with a solution to this wedding situation. No way was he going to be the Chapman failure again. He needed an idea, and quick.

"Is it so wrong that I want a few bambini in the house?"

He rolled his eyes and stepped backward. "No, there's

nothing wrong with that. But I won't play happy families. You'll have to wait until Gracie gets knocked up."

"Don't say knocked up." She scowled.

"I gotta run." He turned, shoving a hand into one pocket to fish around for his car keys.

"Wait!" She scurried back into the kitchen and returned with a cardboard tray filled with plastic containers and glass jars. "I made sauce and some sweets. Chocolate cannoli and *kraffen*."

"The apricot ones?" His tastebuds were already cheering for the delicious doughnut-like pastries.

"Of course." She sent him away with another guilt trip about settling down and finding a wife.

By the time he arrived at First the sun beat down in full force. His leather jacket felt like a straightjacket, stifling him, so he stripped it off and threw it onto the back seat. With a cardboard tray of food balanced in the crook of one arm, he stepped out into the sunshine and kicked the car door closed behind him.

"It's already crazy in there." A voice caught his attention as he walked toward First.

Noah leaned against the side of the restaurant, shielding his eyes with one arm. He looked as though he'd been put through the wringer.

"Busy?"

"Yep. Totally nuts." Noah shook his head. "You're going to be in for a treat tonight."

Great. Fridays were crazy enough anyway with several of the office buildings in the block using First as their after-work watering hole. There were also a few clubs in the area, which meant they got a lot of younger customers having dinner and pre-drinks before a big night out. Fridays were rowdy, and normally he thrived on the hustle and bustle of a busy night's trade, but today his energy was failing him.

Probably because his head was filled with a confusing mix of his pregnant ex and the redhead from last week.

"Excellent," he said, not bothering to hide the sarcasm.

"Oh, more treats from Mama Chapman?" Noah peered into the box and fell into step beside Paul.

"Don't even think about swiping any of this."

The bottles and containers were labeled with sticky notes and his mother's looping, barely legible cursive. Most of the bottles were labelled Des or Paul, but sure enough there was a bottle of pasta sauce and a container of pastries that had "Noah" written on it.

"Score!" Noah reached in and grabbed his items, halting Paul so suddenly that the tray wobbled precariously.

He was about to let out a string of expletives when his attention caught a colorful flash.

"Tiger!" he called out, shoving the tray into Noah's hands.

Libby turned, shaking her head at him. "I told you not to call me that."

She had a box in her hands, a folder sticking out the top. Her mass of copper hair was piled onto her head in a way that looked messy and yet totally perfect. A bright red dress skimmed the tops of her knees, swirling in the light breeze. Again she wore stupidly high heels that looked sexy as all hell.

"How's the ankle?" He looked pointedly at her shoes.

Her lips melted into a sheepish smile. "I was housebound for a few days but there wasn't any permanent damage...just a big dent in my pride."

"And yet I see you haven't learned anything about choosing appropriate footwear for walking down the street." He wandered over to her and lifted the box from her hands. "Let me carry that for you."

"Don't you have your own things to worry about?" She gestured at Noah.

"Nah, he can handle that." Bottles of vodka with girlie logos on the front filled the box he'd taken from her. "I assume this is your product."

"You assume correctly," she said as they walked, her heels clicking on the pavement. "I had a meeting with your brother."

"And?"

She gave him the thumbs down signal. "No good."

"Why?"

His brother was a huge champion for local business. In fact, he stocked several beers from Victorian craft breweries, and he ordered a chunk of his morning pastries from a woman who ran a catering business out of her home. Why not give Libby a chance?

"I don't think he feels that these type of cocktails suit the clientele." She sighed. "He was very polite, but I didn't get much out of him."

"That sounds like my brother." He shook his head. "I can talk to him for you."

They stopped beside a bright red car, and Libby fished around in her bag for her keys. "You would?"

"Of course."

She opened the side door and bent over the backseat, pushing boxes to the other side. Red fabric stretched across the perfect curve of her ass as she leaned forward, sending

Paul's pulse skyrocketing. Teetering on her heels, she wiggled backward and braced her hand on the car door as she stood.

"You don't know me from a bar of soap." She pushed a stray strand of hair from her eyes and bit down on her cherry-colored lip.

"Des doesn't, either. It's possibly why he wasn't keen to get your product in." Paul lowered the box to her backseat and shut the door. "He tends to keep things in the community. All the key employees at First are people he knows and a lot of our suppliers are connections he's made through friends and family."

"I understand." She nodded, sighing. "But I'll be honest, I'm desperate. I've met with a ton of places this week, and all I'm getting is no, no, no. Getting showcased here would mean the world to me."

The frankness in her tone hit him square in the chest. He wanted to help her more than anything and he couldn't explain why, but his instincts told him to believe in her. For the longest time he'd avoided getting to know any women. He didn't want to know about their lives or their problems. But something about Libby had changed that. He *would* help her.

But there was still the problem of getting Des to feel the same way.

"Maybe I could try again, I mean, I know he doesn't have any connection with me but—"

An idea hit Paul like a bolt of lightning, the perfect solution to her problem—and his. "But you *could* have a connection to him."

"How could I do that?"

"This is going to sound crazy. But hear me out."

Libby leaned against the car and nodded. "Crazy is my specialty these days."

"We can get together. Then, as my girlfriend, you can get to know Des and gain his trust."

She arched an eyebrow. "You're right, that's completely crazy. Why would you date me just so I can get to know your brother for the sake of business?"

"We wouldn't really be dating. I'm not the relationship type." Even the thought of it made him itch; he would *not* revisit the pain of what Sadie put him through ever again. "I have zero interest in settling down, but my family is on my back and Des is getting married soon. I don't want to deal with the questions about why I'm not getting married, too."

She didn't need to know about the issue of him facing his ex.

"Why is being single such a bad thing?"

"It's an Italian thing." He shrugged. "Getting married means I'm taking life seriously."

"Because that means grandkids won't be far away?"

"Exactly." He raked a hand through his hair. "At least if I find someone who can pop out grandkids I'll be good for something, according to them."

"I'm not going to have your babies." Libby shook her head, laughing.

"Good, because babies sound like a perfectly good way to ruin my life. I have to get this wedding out of the way and then I can figure out how to avoid the problem permanently. Maybe I'll move to Siberia."

Libby grinned. "It's nice to know that I'm not the only one with a crazy family."

"Think about it. We'll pretend to be dating, so you can

come along to our family dinners and get to know Des. You can convince him to stock your line and then we conveniently break up after the wedding."

And in the meantime he'll come up with a solution to his lackluster career in time to make the necessary changes before the wedding. Simple.

"No babies?" She smirked.

"Absolutely no babies. Nothing real. This will be a completely fake relationship, and you don't have to do anything for me except come along to a few family functions."

Chewing on her lower lip, Libby narrowed her eyes in thought. "Right."

This was totally and utterly crazy…and brilliant. It would solve both their problems and he would have time to figure out what to do with his life. Plus, there was no way in hell he was going to face his ex at the wedding alone. He needed a gorgeous woman on his arm and at least four fingers of scotch before he could deal with that.

"Okay," she said.

"Okay?"

"I have a feeling I'll regret this." Shaking her head, she put a hand on his arm. "But yes…I'll be your fake girlfriend."

Giddiness swept through Libby, though she wasn't sure if it was her body rebelling against the craziness of Paul's idea or the fact that touching him had all but lit her on fire. She'd remembered how it felt having him carry her more than she cared to admit. Now he was in her space again, and his closeness made her legs wobble like jelly.

But she didn't mix business with pleasure, and a fake relationship was the *only* kind of relationship she was interested in.

Especially since his friend had made it clear he wasn't exactly the conservative type when it came to women. The last thing she needed was to get emotionally entangled with another playboy like her last boyfriend. She would *not* be chewed up and spat out by a man ever again.

"Deal?" She stuck her hand out and he took it, wrapping his fingers around hers and sending a frisson of excitement zipping through her.

Okay, he's hot. No big deal, you can handle it. Ignore, ignore, ignore.

"Deal."

"So how exactly does this work?" she asked, pushing a tendril of hair out of her eyes. "I can't say I'm well acquainted with fake relationships."

She wasn't exactly well acquainted with *real* relationships, either, unless you could call a weeklong fling a relationship. Libby had thought she was in a relationship once, she'd even thought that she might have been in love…what a joke.

Now she preferred her men like her cocktails—good-looking, strong, and for weekend and emergency use only.

"We pretend that it's been going on for a while and now we've decided to go public."

"We'll need to do a little cramming for that." She forced the past from her mind and switched on business mode. "I need to know enough about you that people will believe we've been dating. I don't want to get caught out in front of your family."

"Good idea."

"We also need to establish some ground rules for this non-relationship."

He let out a throaty laugh. "Like what?"

"No emotions. This is a business deal." She folded her arms across her chest. "You're not allowed to fall in love with me."

"Libby, you're gorgeous but there's no chance in hell of that happening. Sorry to burst your bubble," he said without sounding sorry at all. "I don't do love."

As much as she was relieved at his agreement, her mind wanted to focus on the "you're gorgeous" part.

"No sex."

"Fine."

"With anyone," she clarified. "We're not going to be sleeping together, but I don't want you getting caught with another girl and making me look like a fool."

"I'm not a cheater," he said, his face unreadable though a muscle twitched in his jaw. "Anything else?"

"I think that's it. Anything you want to add?"

"So long as it looks real enough that my family buys it, I'm happy. I hope you're a good actress, Tiger."

"I can be very convincing when I want to be." She tipped her nose up in the air and narrowed her eyes at him. "And if you call me Tiger again I'm going to make you regret it."

Paul tilted his head and looked at her in a way that could only be described as predatory. "How do you plan on doing that?"

"I'll make you want to break one of those rules. I'll leave it up to you to guess which one."

"I don't like your chances." He stepped closer, the breadth of his shoulders dwarfing her. "But I'm happy to play."

"Just make it easy for yourself and call me Libby, okay?" She smiled sweetly and stood her ground.

"Easy, Tiger. I'll play nice." His dark chocolate eyes assessed her, smoothing her up and down as though committing her proportions to memory.

His gaze smoldered, so intense her body reacted instantly. The clench of her sex sent a sharp jolt of arousal through her, pebbling her nipples and sending warm, throbbing heat through her veins.

Damn him.

"Why don't you come by my place over the weekend and we can do a 'getting to know you' catch up." She reached into her purse and pulled out a business card and a pen, desperate to keep her body focused on something other than how Paul affected her.

"Done." He smiled, revealing a perfect set of white teeth.

At one point she would have fallen head over heels for a smile like that, but now she knew better. The gorgeous ones always made you pay with more than you could afford. They were like credit card debt: trouble from the beginning and hard to get over. Business, however, was business, and she intended to make full use of this situation. First would be the *perfect* place to launch Libby Gal Cocktails—their write up in Gastronomy Magazine had been glowing, and that meant interest from food bloggers and the media.

She *had* to make this work.

"Here's my address, my phone and email are on the front of the card. Does Sunday afternoon work?" Her intuitive senses tingled. She knew a good opportunity when she saw it. All she needed now was to convince Des Chapman to take her on…and make sure she kept her hands off his brother.

Chapter Four

Libby checked herself out in the mirror for what felt like the hundredth time that afternoon. She'd put far too much effort into making herself look as though she hadn't expended any effort at all.

But her curls were artfully mussed, and she'd fiddled with the hem of her black and white striped shirt until it looked as though she'd thrown it on without a care. Her faded jeans were frayed in places, though she doubted Paul would realize they'd been designed that way. All she had to do now was dab a little red lipstick on and slip her feet into a pair of ballet flats.

Why are you so worked up? This is a fake *relationship remember…it doesn't matter what he thinks of you.*

The doorbell sounded as Libby hunted for her second shoe. She found it sticking out from under the couch in her living room and hopped on one foot while she slipped it on.

Taking a deep breath, she gathered herself before

opening the door.

"I was starting to think you weren't home," Paul said, amusement dancing in his tone. "Were you still getting ready?"

"Getting ready?" She rolled her eyes as though it was the stupidest comment in the world. "I was working."

"Right." His eyes raked over her. "May I come in?"

Heat crawled up her cheeks until she was sure they were the same color as her shoes. She stepped aside and held the door open. "Of course."

He walked into the living room, affording her the chance to linger on the way his dark jeans perfectly outlined his legs and butt. He wore a dark gray T-shirt this time, instead of black. A faint whiff of aftershave clung to the air around him, something woodsy and masculine.

So he'd put in a little effort, too…or maybe he just woke up looking and smelling like sex personified.

She smiled, forcing the inappropriate thoughts aside. "Welcome to my humble abode."

"I wouldn't call it humble." He turned around, eyes sweeping over her antique sideboard and the custom coffee table she'd bought in Italy a few years ago. "It's great."

"Thank you." The compliment warmed her insides.

Do I need to remind you not to care about his opinion?

"Can I get you a drink?" she asked, suddenly needing to keep her hands busy.

He had a vibe that screamed at her to touch him, which would be highly inappropriate. Especially considering they were about to plot out how to fool his whole family into thinking they were in love.

"A coffee would be great." He followed her into the kitchen and leaned against the breakfast counter. "Black, no sugar."

"Why doesn't that surprise me?" She reached up onto her tiptoes to fish out an espresso cup from the top shelf.

From the corner of her eye she noticed Paul watching her, his lips pressed together lightly. Hands jammed into the front pockets of his jeans, drawing far too much attention to the way the denim molded to every inch of him…and she was sure there would be plenty of inches.

"I don't drink that syrupy gingerbread latte crap, if that's what you mean." He grinned. "I think I'd be stripped of my heritage if I did."

"You're Italian, right? I think you mentioned that," she said as though she hadn't analyzed every single word from their previous conversation. Setting the espresso cup down next to a pink and gold floral mug, she smiled. They looked a little ridiculous side by side.

"Half. My ma is Italian but my dad's Australian. What about you? I'm guessing you're English or Irish with all that red hair."

The coffee machine came to life and steam hissed out of the milk-frothing nozzle. "English, although I believe there is a bit of Scottish mixed in as well. My grandparents immigrated a few years after the second world war."

"Good to know." He nodded. "So we should cover the basics. Favorite foods, movies, color…sex positions."

She shot him a reproachful look and held the espresso cup under the machine's spout. Dark liquid filled the air with a delicious aroma, the coffee mingling with the tempting scent of his aftershave. Heat coursed through her, her head spinning.

"I was kidding about the sex positions, although if you

want to enlighten me I'm all ears." A cheeky grin spread over his face, making his dark eyes sparkle.

Yeah, he would have women lining up with that naughtiness. All the better to remind her why she shouldn't get emotionally involved.

"You've got no chance of that. But I can tell you my favorite color is green, my favorite movie is *Die Hard*, and I eat pretty much anything."

"*Die Hard*." He looked impressed. "The first one?"

"Of course, it's a classic." She handed him the coffee cup and turned back to the machine to froth milk for her cappuccino. "But I do love the third one, too. Jeremy Irons is a great villain."

"Did you see the fifth one?"

"Yes, but I pretend that I didn't. In my mind they stopped at three." She grinned and poured the hot milk into her coffee. "What about you?"

"My favorite color is black."

"Black isn't a color."

"If I can buy a T-shirt in it, it's a color." He took a sip of his coffee. "Favorite movie is *Pulp Fiction* and I love Italian food. Obviously."

"Can you cook?"

"A bit. Not that I need to, I get plied with home-cooked food. My freezer is full of pasta sauce and soup."

"That must be nice." She took a long gulp of her coffee to hide her jealousy.

He nodded, averting his gaze for a moment. "Speaking of my family, you'll get to meet them tonight."

"*Tonight*?" she squeaked.

"Yeah, we're doing a family dinner. I'm bringing you

along to meet them. It'll be a good time to introduce you to everyone."

She rolled her eyes. "Thanks for telling me."

"You're welcome."

"I was being sarcastic! We don't know anything about each other yet." She grappled for an excuse. "How do you know I'm not busy?"

He cocked his head. "Are you?"

"Well…no." She sighed. "You should have given me more notice."

He shrugged. "It's not a big deal. We were planning to talk through everything today so at least it will all be fresh in your mind tonight. Besides, I thought this was what you wanted."

She blew an errant strand of hair out of her eyes with a huff. Getting her brand into Des's bar was what she wanted, fronting up to his family…well, that was her end of the bargain. But it made her insides twist and turn. She wasn't very good when it came to playing happy family. Still, a promise was a promise.

"Okay, fine. What else do I need to know about you?"

"I don't bring girls home to meet my parents."

"Ever?"

"Once." He swallowed and looked as though he was about to explain, but a shield seemed to shoot up around him. "You'll be the first one in quite a while. As I said, I don't do relationships."

"Me, either."

"Really?" He raised a brow. "Why?"

"My parents had a crappy marriage and Dad's now on to wife number four or five. I tried once to have a relationship."

She paused. "It didn't end well."

"That's a shame."

"No it's not. Don't tell me you're one of those guys who think all girls are waiting to trap a man into marriage." She wrinkled her nose. "I'm perfectly happy without the wedding, the white picket fence, and the commitment."

He chuckled. "Music to my ears."

She sipped her coffee and motioned for Paul to follow her into the living area. "I can support myself and, so long as other needs are taken care of, I'm perfectly happy being independent."

"And what *other needs* might they be?" He dropped down onto the couch, crossing an ankle over one knee.

He seemed to take up all the room, and Libby forced herself not to admire how damned delectable he looked sprawled out like that. She chose an armchair on the opposite side of the coffee table. Better to keep a little distance.

"None that you need to worry about," she said, crossing her legs demurely.

"Have you got a rabbit for that?"

"A rabbit?" She opened her mouth to ask him what he meant and then snapped it shut when the true meaning of his words settled over her. "What I do in the privacy of my own home is none of your business."

"I need to know my *girlfriend* isn't left wanting." He grinned at her like a wolf sizing up its prey.

"I'm perfectly fine, thank you."

"So why did your relationship end badly? Some bastard hurt you?" He drummed his fingers on his knee, his eyes narrowed.

"Yes."

Some bastard had used and discarded her like a take-away coffee cup…casting her out of the one place where she'd wanted acceptance. Craved it. Needed it with the desperation of a starving woman reaching for food because she'd *never* been able to get it at home. But she'd failed and had been humiliated for it.

That was her punishment for thinking she could change a womanizer into a reliable, committed partner.

The memory still bit into her, sharp and painful. But it had been a lesson she needed to learn, so Libby did the same as any good student would do. She copped the failure on the chin and adjusted her behavior accordingly.

No relationships, no commitment, no emotions. Just a little fun when she needed it, so long as she was sure she could keep the other person at arm's length. Flings were better than relationships, anyway—it was the honeymoon period without any of the crap that followed.

"What did he do?" he asked, the curiosity undisguised in his voice.

"It's not relevant."

Paul nodded. Sunlight shone into the room between the slats of her blinds, casting a flickering light as the breeze from an open window pushed them around. He hadn't shaved—the dark stubble made the angle of his jaw look even sharper and more appealing.

Libby distracted herself by inspecting her freshly manicured nails for imperfections. "What's your family like?"

"They can be a little intense." He raked a hand through his hair, but the dark waves sprung stubbornly back into place. "But they're good people. Traditional. My ma will be very excited when you turn up for dinner."

"You haven't told her I'm coming?" She blinked.

"I thought we'd go with the element of surprise."

She could just imagine how her father would react if she randomly turned up at his house with a man. Then again, the chances of Paul's family being anything like her own were slim. Like runway model slim.

"How do you think they'll take it?" She guarded her tone, hoping he wouldn't pick up on the hint of insecurity that grew inside her like a weed. But she needed to prepare mentally if he was going to feed her to the sharks.

"Are you kidding?" He bobbed his head. "They'll think the sun shines out of your ass."

Laughter bubbled in her throat at his choice of metaphor. "Why?"

"Because you're girlie and sweet, but you look like you don't take any shit from anyone, either." His eyes lingered on her. "Besides, who wouldn't think you were the perfect girl for their son?"

"I don't know." She sipped her coffee, her hands cradling the colorful mug. "This is a first for me, too. I don't meet a guy's parents if I can help it."

"So I'm popping your cherry, then?"

"I'm serious about making my business work, and I'll do whatever it takes," she said, ignoring the innuendo.

"I can see that." Paul's expression was guarded, his dark eyes revealing nothing as he interlaced his fingers behind his head.

The pose made his biceps bulge beneath the soft cotton of his T-shirt. As it pulled across his chest, Libby's eyes drifted to the muscles there. He was so…defined.

"So how did we meet?" she asked, dragging her eyes up

to his face.

Paul smirked. "Can't we go with the truth? I picked you up at a bar."

She shook her head. "No. We met through a friend of a friend, some loose connection no one will ask about."

"Boring."

"Believable. We don't need to be interesting, in fact, the less interesting the better." She tucked a loose strand of hair behind her ear. "We want to seem as normal and unexciting as possible."

"You're making our relationship sound like wholegrain cereal."

She smirked. "Trust me, the less information you give people the easier lying is."

"You can try that, but my mother puts gossip reporters to shame. Trust me."

Pulling up into his parents' driveway with Libby in the passenger seat was weird to say the least. For a guy who'd been called so laidback he could barely stand, he suddenly felt as jittery as a teenager on a first date. Maybe it was because he remembered the exact moment he'd brought Sadie home. While she wasn't as vibrant and confident as Libby, she'd had that same polish about her. Perfect hair, perfect clothes, perfect smile.

She's not Sadie, and this is not a real relationship. Relax.

In the close confines of the car Libby's delicious scent intoxicated him. She smelled like roses and those pink musk candies he'd devoured as a kid. Sweet, heavenly, and utterly addictive.

"Is there anything else you want to ask me before we go in?" She fiddled with the mirror on the passenger side visor, touching a pink gloss to her lips.

"I think we're good." He turned, reaching through to the back seat to grab his jacket.

Libby's throat was inches from his face as his hand groped along the back seat. Her breath stuttered in the silence of the car. Was it his imagination, or did her eyes look a little wider?

"Great." Her voice came out tight, her smile overbright.

He touched his hand to her arm and immediately regretted it. "We'll be fine. You've got nothing to worry about."

The soft cotton of her top was so thin he could feel the heat radiating from her skin. Her breath hitched before she opened the passenger side door with a little more force than was necessary.

"I'm not worried. Not even a little bit."

Outside, he shrugged into his jacket. Had he totally lost his mind? Bringing a fake girlfriend home to meet the family was a low move. His mother would fall in love with Libby, he knew that for sure. Talk about giving her false hope.

He swallowed down the desire to turn around and take Libby back to her house. As much as he loved his family, it was their fault he'd been put in this situation. If they didn't put so much pressure on him to be like his brother he wouldn't feel the need to lie…would he?

He forced himself to think of the wedding, of the years of criticism and scrutiny his aunts and uncles had heaped on him. Of all the things they'd said to his mother under the guise of being "helpful." He forced himself to think of Sadie, pregnant with his cousin's child.

The child *he'd* once dreamed of having.

Bringing a fake girlfriend home might be low, but he wasn't a cheating son of a bitch like his cousin. Still, he felt like a dick doing this to his family. Especially his ma.

"Let's go," he said, holding out his arm to Libby. "It's showtime."

She stood taller against him, having changed into a pair of her signature crazy-high heels. As much as he knew his relationship with Libby was fake, he couldn't help imagining what she'd look like in *only* those heels. Like dessert and heaven and sex rolled into one, he'd bet.

Her hand rested lightly on his arm, her body pushed against him. She teetered on the unsteady paving of his parents' front steps. Each bump of her hip sent a shot of heat through him.

He'd spent the afternoon trying not to think about how attractive she was with that mane of red hair and that perky butt encased in faded denim. In all likelihood he'd failed but, judging by some of the looks she'd thrown him, the feeling was mutual.

"You're asking for trouble in those shoes," he said, forcing his attention to something safer than Libby's distracting curves.

"I'm asking for trouble anyway." She offered him a sly smile as he rang the doorbell. "The shoes are just the cherry on top."

Paul was about to ask her what kind of trouble she preferred when a thumping noise came from the house followed by footsteps. "You're not scared of dogs, are you?"

Libby's eyes widened as she stepped toward the door.

"Not really…I don't think."

At that moment the front door burst open and the Chapmans' very large, very excited Great Dane burst forth. He immediately locked onto Libby and jumped up, throwing his paws over her shoulders.

"Oh my God!" She wobbled on her heels, but Paul grabbed her around the waist from behind, preventing her from toppling over and taking the dog with her.

She stumbled back against him, her ass pushing squarely against his groin as she tried to wriggle free from the dog's grip. If she hadn't known about his attraction to her before, she would now.

Trust his libido to come back in full force with the one girl who had a "no sex" policy.

"Down, Cavallo!" His mother's voice rang out over the commotion. *"Siediti!"*

The dog relinquished, its large tail thumping against the doorframe. Even seated, the top of his head came up to the bottom of Libby's ribcage. Cavallo sniffed her and then proceeded to wipe a long strip of doggy drool across her jeans.

"I am so sorry," his mother said, shooing the dog inside. "He gets very excited when we have guests."

"It's okay." Libby blinked, looking down at her jeans and then back up to Paul, stifling a smile. "Excitement is a natural thing."

Paul tried to subtly adjust the front of his jeans so his hard-on wouldn't be noticeable, but the quick flick of Libby's eyes told him he'd been well and truly sprung.

"Ma, this is Libby…my girlfriend." It couldn't have come out any more awkward if he'd tried, but the tension would be lost on his mother. Hopefully so would the guilty tone in his voice.

She looked pleased as punch as she held the door open and motioned for them to come inside. "I'm Leone, so lovely to meet you."

"Sorry to spring this on you. I understand Paul didn't let you know I was coming." Libby shot Paul a mock-stern look.

"Not to worry. We always have plenty of food." His mother smiled warmly and patted Paul on the cheek.

He could practically feel the excitement shimmering off her. "Don't make this a big deal, Ma," he said into her ear.

What the hell was he doing? This was his family, his blood. And he was going to parade Libby around like some kind of magician's trick. A diversion tactic while he tried to make something of himself in the background. Clearly, he hadn't been thinking. But it was too late now. His ma was trying her hardest not to burst into a huge smile as she closed the door behind them. "Your brother and Gracie are already here, go through to the table. Dinner will be out in a few minutes."

"Is there anything I can do to help?" Libby asked. "I feel bad we didn't bring a bottle of wine or anything with us."

"Ma won't let us bring anything to dinner," Paul said.

"It's fine, I'm nearly done. You two take a seat and get something to drink." Her dark eyes shone as she gave one more pointed look at him before she bustled off down the hallway.

"You could have warned me about the dog," Libby said, looking down at her jeans.

Cavallo milled around, still intent on sniffing out the new person in the house. Libby reached out and tentatively scratched his head, her shoulders relaxing when she realized the big beast wanted a little affection and not a bite of her hand.

"What's her name?" she asked.

"His," Paul corrected. "Cavallo. It means horse in Italian."

"Fitting." She laughed. "You could have warned me about something else, too."

"I have no idea what you're talking about."

"Bull." Her hazel eyes glittered. "I thought we agreed no sex."

"We agreed not to have it, but there's not a chance in hell of me not thinking about it."

A pink flush crawled up her cheeks, and she kept quiet. They spent a few more minutes fussing over the dog, and Paul found a tissue so Libby could clean up her jeans.

His mother's voice carried through the house, her excited Italian revealing to the others that Paul had brought a girl to dinner. Thankfully, Libby seemed to have no idea what was going on. As if on cue, Gracie poked her head out from the dining room, and a big grin spread across her face. No doubt Des had translated his mother's pronouncement to her.

"Hello!" She bounded out and gave Paul a quick hug. "Who's this?"

"Gracie, meet Libby."

"Welcome," Gracie said, sticking her hand out.

The girls shook hands. "Nice to meet you."

Gracie motioned for them to come through to the dining room, turning back to wink at Paul when Libby couldn't see. Des and their father were already seated at the table, both of them subtly raising a brow when Paul ushered Libby inside.

The introductions went round the table with lightning

efficiency, and then the food appeared. Over the clattering of cutlery, serving spoons, and appreciative full-mouthed grumbles, Paul watched as Libby drank it all in with wide eyes.

"So, Libby, I had no idea you were dating my brother. How long have you two been going out?" Des asked, though the implication in his question was *why is this the first we've heard about it.*

"Not that long," Libby replied, reaching for her glass of water and taking a big gulp. "We only made it official recently."

Gracie leaned forward, her curiosity undisguised. "And how did you meet?"

"Through a friend of a friend." She nodded as though convincing herself, but she made a show of squeezing Paul's shoulder affectionately. "We hit it off right away, something about him felt...perfect."

"That's so sweet." Gracie looked to Des. "Remember when we were like that?"

Des nodded. "We're *still* like that."

"Tell us a little about yourself, Libby." His mother said, gesturing with a forkful of broccoli. "Since my son has told us nothing."

The excitement in her voice twisted like a knife in his stomach. What would happen when he and Libby "broke up" after the wedding? Would she go back to thinking that he'd failed her? What if she found out he'd been lying the whole time? He couldn't let that happen.

Having Libby by his side would help for now, but it was only one part of the plan. He needed to figure out the rest of it before he ended up in a worse position than where he started.

Chapter Five

Libby felt every pair of eyes in the room turn to her in the wake of Leone's question. The clacking of cutlery stopped, and Paul's entire family waited expectantly.

"Well," she said, taking a deep breath. "There's not much to say. I'm an only child, I was studying medicine, but I've put my schooling on hold to work on a business venture. I love to travel."

Was meeting a prospective partner's parents always like this? It felt like an awkward job interview and she hated running off the aspects of her life like items on a grocery list. She shifted in her seat, her eyes darting to Paul silently begging him for help.

"Her favorite movie is *Die Hard*," Paul added.

"The first one?" Paul's father, Darren, asked. It was the first thing he'd said all evening.

Libby smiled. "Of course."

"You know, I don't know why they made the fourth and

fifth ones," he said, shaking his head. The older man had dark hair with a smattering of gray around the temples, he wore thin wire-rimmed glasses and, though he looked like the stern silent type, his face lit up at the change of conversation. "I didn't see them."

Libby's shoulders relaxed. "You didn't miss much. I mean, I love Bruce Willis, but you need to know when something has jumped the shark."

"Exactly!" Darren thumped the table with his fist, making the salt and pepper shakers jump.

The table dissolved into a debate about the prevalence of sequels in action cinema, which lead to an argument about the reboot of Indiana Jones. Libby and Darren were clearly on the same side, while Gracie and Des argued against them.

Paul sat back quietly, tucking into his food though his eyes kept darting over to her. Even silent, his presence radiated, drawing her attention away from everything else... including the dance-in-your-mouth delights that his mother had placed on the table.

Thinking about the way his body had felt pressed up against her would lead to trouble, but how could she forget the hardness of his muscles—and other things—against the curve of her back, and his hands at her waist. He was masculine without being macho, strong without being forceful. The perfect balance.

"If you keep staring at me like that I'll have to take you home," he whispered, placing his hand on her thigh under the table.

The rest of the table chatted amongst themselves. Libby scanned the room to see if anyone was watching them. "I'm not staring...and keep your hands to yourself."

"But we're supposed to be dating." His breath warmed her neck, sending a tingle of anticipation skittering down her spine.

"And you like to feel up all your dates with your parents sitting not three feet away?"

"You're the first one I've brought home in a long time, remember? I've forgotten how it works."

She swallowed, ignoring how close his lips were. If she turned her head she'd catch them with her own. "Me, too."

His hand remained on her thigh, the heat from his palm matching the fire that had started to slow-burn low down in her belly. He traced shapes on her leg, every so often inching his hand farther up her thigh. She could have easily knocked him away, but the insistent throbbing in her sex overrode her desire to be sensible.

"Are you sure you want me to stop?"

His aftershave filled her nostrils as he leaned a little closer, his hand mere inches from where she wanted to be touched. So close and yet the distance seemed unbearable— her body cried out for him to stroke her. To explore her.

She cleared her throat as she noticed that the conversation had died down at the table. Interlacing her fingers with Paul's, she drew his hand away, relieved and devastated at the same time.

"We should clear the dishes," she said to Paul, loudly enough that he wouldn't be able to back out of it.

Without waiting for his agreement, she pushed up from her chair and collected the empty plates.

"You don't need to do that," Leone said, reaching out to stop her.

"Please, it's the least I can do. You accommodated me

without any notice at all, I'd like to help." She sent Paul's mother her most charming smile, and the older woman sat back down, a pleased expression on her face.

Okay, so maybe she was better with families than she first thought.

Although it was clear that the Chapmans were nothing like her own family. The conversation was filled with in-jokes, playful teasing, and all the love she'd wished for as a little kid. In only one evening she could see herself being part of this family, being accepted and loved and cherished.

All the more reason to make sure you remember the point of this "relationship." It's business and you're lying to these people, which means you can't get involved.

Paul followed her, stacking the empty plates and bowls as expertly as he did at the bar. "You're such a girl scout," he said as they walked into the kitchen, a smirk tugging at his full lips.

They opened the dishwasher and began to rinse and load the crockery. "I was raised to have manners."

The kitchen was small, and they stood next to each other, working together as though they'd done it a thousand times before. Their rhythms matched as if on some basal level they understood the other person's movements and habits. Paul reached past Libby to grab a plate, brushing her ribcage with his knuckles.

"Hands off," she admonished, though she was starting to mean it less and less.

"You seemed to enjoy it when I had my hands on you before." His eyes swept over her, his lips wearing that predatory smile again.

The same smile she knew would feature in her dreams

if she didn't shut this attraction down now. "And how could you tell that?"

"You got this look on your face." He leaned closer to her. "Your eyes got all wide and I could feel your thighs clenching."

Her face flushed hard and fast. "You could not."

"Could so. You wanted me to keep going."

She grappled for a protest but none came to her lips. He was right. "Regardless, we have an agreement."

"That's the best you can do?" He laughed, cocky and as sure of himself as a guy who was used to charming women out of their pants. "Are you telling me you're not attracted to me?"

It was no use lying, she wasn't the best at hiding her feelings anyway. "I didn't say that, but it's beside the point."

"Why?"

She looked behind her to make sure they were alone. "Because this is a business arrangement, nothing more. I don't want things to get messy."

Messy was an understatement. She didn't want to get used and discarded for a newer model the way she had back in university. The way her father had done to her mother years before that.

History *would* repeat itself if she wasn't careful, and Paul would only be able to use her if she let him. But she wouldn't. Their arrangement gave her something precious—an opportunity, a chance—and she would otherwise keep him at a distance.

"But getting messy is so much fun." He reached out to her and pulled her to him, his hips flat against her belly as he wedged her against the kitchen bench. "Besides, they're spying on us."

"Who?"

"My family." He inclined his head back toward the kitchen door with a movement so subtle she felt as though they were spies communicating undercover. "We should sell it; we don't want them thinking this is *just business.*"

His hands touched her hips, his fingers tracing the line at the top of her jeans just under her shirt. The throbbing started up again, insistent. Demanding.

"They don't think that," she protested, but her hands came up to his chest as if controlled by a puppet master tugging her strings.

His muscles were hard beneath her palms, and she had to stop herself from rubbing against him. Out of the corner of her eyes she saw a flash of red. Gracie.

"Okay, maybe they *are* watching us."

"Ready to play the part?" One hand came up to cup the angle of her jaw. "Let's see what kind of actress you are."

"This is purely for show," she said, the breath rushing out of her lungs as his face hovered close to hers.

"Of course." His lips brushed the space next to the corner of her mouth, so close and yet the distance felt like pure, unadulterated torture. "You won't enjoy this at all."

"I won't."

Liar, liar, pants on fire.

He angled her head, coming down over her in a way that was completely possessive and in control. As his lips parted hers, she sighed against him, her body losing the ability to hold itself upright. Every nerve ending in her body sparkled like New Year's fireworks, and her fists curled into his T-shirt.

The moment his tongue touched hers her mind went

blank, the taste of wine on his lips and the scent of his skin driving her to a point of desperation. His fingers thrust into her hair, pulling her head back so he could take more, demand more. Taste more.

Unable to stop herself, Libby pressed her hips against him, gently rubbing up and down until a wonderfully guttural sound came from the back of his throat. He was hard beneath her hands, the muscles in his chest perfectly shaped. The press of his thighs against hers enough to spark wild images in her mind.

"You seem fairly invested," he murmured against her lips, pulling away from the kiss with a dark fire in his eyes, "for someone who's not enjoying herself."

"Just playing the part." The crack in her voice betrayed just how much she'd wanted that kiss to continue.

"Right." A cocky smile passed over his lips as he nudged her legs apart with his thigh.

A small gasp came rushing out as he pressed against the distracting ache there. If they'd been alone her restraint would have shattered like glass against stone. Thank God his family was in the next room.

"You don't look like you want to jump me at all," he teased.

"I'm a good actress." Sucking in a breath, Libby pressed her lips together and straightened up. "That's what you wanted, isn't it?"

"It's one thing I want."

Paul was not a guy who would be easily fooled. She'd have to be more careful about how much she revealed around him. She'd already made it clear she was attracted to him, but her business came first.

That was one thing she *didn't* have to pretend.

"Your family is waiting," she said primly. "You don't want them to think I'm some floozy who's ready to jump their son in the next room."

"I don't much care what they think, you just say the word." He brushed his hand down the side of her neck, tracing her collarbone with a fingertip.

"You *should* care." She wriggled out of his grasp and closed the door to the dishwasher. "You have a family who loves you. If you don't care about that you don't deserve them."

A moment later, when they'd no doubt decided that the kissing had stopped, Leone entered the kitchen. "How about some dessert?"

"Why didn't Libby mention anything about being your girlfriend when she met with me the other day?" Des asked, leaning back in his chair and rolling up the sleeves on his shirt. The bottom of one tattoo peeked out. The colored ink looked even more intense against the white cotton.

"We hadn't decided that we were going to go public yet." Paul shrugged, pretending to inspect his coffee so he didn't have to face his brother's doubt. Or the churning in his own gut. "She wanted to come to you on her own so you'd focus on her business idea rather than seeing her as my girlfriend."

The lie tasted sour on his tongue. Paul was many things but he'd always been an open book. Lying wasn't something that felt natural, but he reminded himself why he and Libby had entered into this arrangement. He was done being second best.

"I think it's a great idea, but it's not really something that would suit First." Des brushed a hand through his hair, a hint of remorse in his voice. "I feel bad saying no, but I have to do what's best for the business. You know that, right?"

"I know." Paul nodded, watching Libby's red hair glimmer under the lamplight as she sat a few feet away in the lounge room chatting to his mother and Gracie.

"I was pretty abrupt," Des admitted. "But I know when something's right and when it's not."

"It's fine. She's a tough one, I don't think it's the first time she's had to deal with people saying no to her."

Des grimaced. "You should have given me the heads-up."

"Why?"

"It's been a while since you brought anyone home. I'm sure you don't want her to think your family is full of jerks."

"She doesn't think that."

"Good, because I think Ma is already picking out table settings for *your* wedding."

Paul held up his hands. "Let's focus on getting you married. I've got no plans to get hitched anytime soon."

"Anytime soon? That seems like a turnaround from your previous opinion that weddings are a total waste of money and that you'd never even consider it."

Paul swallowed and pushed back the memory of traipsing around the city trying to find the perfect ring for Sadie. He'd picked it out, too, but his credit card had been deactivated that day. The bank had found fraudulent activity on his account, and he couldn't pay for the ring. A stroke of luck that saved him the last of his humiliation. That afternoon he'd come home to find Sadie packing her bags, his smug-faced cousin by her side. The stench of her infidelity seeping into the walls of their apartment.

He'd never told anyone about his plans to propose.

Paul's lips twisted into a grimace. "I haven't changed my mind."

"There's a big difference between not wanting to get hitched *anytime soon* and not wanting it ever." Des folded his arms across his chest and grinned. "She's gotten to you. That's why you brought her home."

"I was quite content keeping my family and my love life separate…"

"But?"

"Libby's…different." At least that wasn't a lie. "She's different from Sadie."

Des chuckled. "You mean she's not a two-faced, cheating waste of space?"

Paul's head snapped up. "I thought you liked Sadie."

He'd never heard a single family member say a bad word about his ex, not even after everything that had happened. Deep down he'd always wondered if they'd wished the two of them had stayed together. Or worse, they blamed him for the breakup…for driving her into another man's arms.

"I liked her well enough while you were going out, but you can't really excuse what she did." Des frowned. "I know Ma always says we have to remember she's still part of the family but…"

"But?"

"She still cheated on you." Des shook his head and clapped a hand down on his shoulder. "That's low."

"Thanks."

"I never knew what to say when it happened, and I thought bringing it up would make it worse."

Paul speared the last piece of his dessert with a fork and popped it into his mouth. "But now that you're all partnered up you can talk about girly shit like that."

His brother smirked. "You're partnered up, too, it won't be long before you have to give your opinion on flowers and champagne and colors. Honestly, I don't know how girls manage to look at three pink things and think they're all different. Salmon, my ass. It's bloody pink."

"They should come with an instruction manual." Paul looked back over to where the girls sat.

Libby threw her head back, laughing at something his mother had said. The tinkling sound sent a shiver through him. At that moment she looked up, her eyes connecting with his. Color spread through her cheeks and her neck, reminding him of how hot she'd felt underneath his hands.

She'd kissed like she meant it. He didn't believe for a second that she was *that* good an actress. He certainly hadn't been acting. The moment her little hands grabbed his T-shirt and she'd thrust her hips up against him he'd gone hard as stone.

Just business. Yeah right.

He was going to convince Libby that her "no sex" rule was pointless. He had absolutely no trouble separating sex from emotion. And if they had to play the part, why not use the real chemistry that already existed between them? It made sense, they'd fool everyone completely. No one would ever suspect it was all for show.

Chapter Six

Libby stared at the calendar on her wall, neat squares with tidy little *X*s in green ink. She'd accumulated seven since her visit to Paul's family dinner. Since she'd set in motion plans to get Libby Gal Cocktails into First. Since she'd kissed Paul.

A whole week and the memory of his lips on hers pulsed within her as though it had happened moments ago.

Distraction plagued her like a dark cloud hovering overhead. Thinking about *that* kiss, being annoyed and forcing herself to think about something else, then thinking about the kiss again.

Nothing dulled the memory, not sleep deprivation from her vivid dreams nor the fact that no other restaurants seemed keen to take her on.

"You're acting like a silly school girl," she said to herself as she paused in front of the ornate mirror in her hallway. "It was just a kiss."

But *oh*, what a kiss it had been. The kind of toe-curling, sigh-inducing, heart-rate-spiking kiss you saw in movies. Paul had a kissing mastery like none she'd experienced before.

"That means he's kissed a lot of girls," she said to her reflection, frowning. "Don't go thinking you're special."

Afternoon sunlight filtered in through the open blinds in her office, causing rainbows to dance in the antique crystal perfume bottles that decorated her bookshelf. She hefted a box of custom stationery that had arrived in the mail that morning. Pink envelopes, matching "with compliments" slips, and swing tags that would never see the light of day if she didn't convince Des to take on her product.

She'd stopped by the restaurant once this week to have coffee with Nina, hoping to catch either Paul or Des. But they'd been out, apparently organizing something for the wedding.

Libby set the box down next to the bookshelf and pulled her phone out of her pocket. No missed calls, no texts. No communication whatsoever from Paul.

It would be okay to call him, wouldn't it? The kiss wasn't real and therefore the rules of dating didn't apply...did they? She shoved the phone back into the pocket of her white sundress.

It was just a kiss, get out of your own head! It didn't mean anything to him, and it shouldn't mean anything to you.

A knock at the front door broke Libby out of her thoughts. She slipped on a pair of beige heels—she was raised never to greet a guest barefoot—and made her way to the front door.

"Hello?" She opened the door with a smile that died on her lips. "Dad."

"Hello, Libby."

Her father towered over her, his physical height nothing compared to the intimidation wrought by his sharp hazel eyes and stern mouth. He wore a sports coat over a white shirt and chinos and, despite the fact that it was sweltering outside, not a drop of perspiration glistened on his skin.

Kirk Harris was ever the cool cucumber, totally in control…even of his sweat glands.

"Please, come in," she said, her stiff lips struggling to get the words out.

"You haven't been taking my calls." He walked past her, looking around the room as though surveying enemy territory.

"I've been busy," she said, letting the door close behind her. "It's nothing personal."

"You don't do anything without purpose, my dear." He clasped his hands behind his back. "Why are you avoiding me?"

"Like I said, I've been busy." She forced herself to appear relaxed. Undaunted.

Shoulders down. No fidgeting. Move slowly as though you have all the time in the world.

Her father sensed fear, so the best thing she could do would be act like everything was peachy. No mean feat, but she'd fooled Paul's parents with her perfect girlfriend act. A flicker of guilt swept through her, but she shoved it aside.

"How is the…" He swallowed. "Business?"

"Don't say business like it's a dirty word, Dad." She rolled her eyes. "I'm making cocktails, not porn."

"I heard you've got a competitor."

"All businesses have competitors." She stood her ground, kept the emotion out of her voice, and maintained eye contact as he'd taught her to do when she needed to deal with a difficult patient.

His gaze swept over the room as if searching for clues that she was failing. "So it hasn't affected you?"

"I've had a few setbacks but nothing I can't handle." She folded her arms across her chest.

"When are you going to give up this charade and go back to your studies? You were so close to finishing." He shrugged out of his jacket and slung it over one arm, picking at some imaginary imperfection in the fabric.

"I'm giving this a shot, Dad. One setback doesn't mean I've failed. I'm not going to run back to med school with my tail between my legs."

"Don't be so stubborn. You had everything laid out before you. I could have gotten you into any hospital in the country."

She turned away from him, trying to control the anger swirling like red mist in front of her eyes. "I'm *not* going back."

"How can you throw away everything I've done for you? All that expensive schooling, the strings I pulled to get you into the best university in the country."

Libby glared at him. "I never asked for your help."

"You're throwing away a bright future for nothing."

"A bright future?" She laughed, the humorless sound echoing in the quiet room. "Will it be filled with failed marriages and abandoned children like yours? If so, I don't want it."

"I never abandoned you."

"I'm twenty-five years old, you can stop lying to me now." Tears pricked the back of her eyelids, much to her disgust.

The angry silence radiated off her father like a toxic fume. "You never wanted for anything growing up. I gave you the best education, the best toys, the best food."

"What I wanted was a mother and father who could stand to be in the same room and who didn't bad-mouth each other."

"Your mother and I divorced years ago, you can't hold that against me." He waved his hand, shooing away her concerns as if they were nothing more than an irritating insect.

"No, especially since it's clear marriage means nothing to you. Speaking of, how is wife number five?"

"Julianna is my *fourth* wife," he said, cold eyes raking over her. "And I will not have you talk to me with such disrespect."

"You turn up unannounced to berate me. What did you expect?" The words rushed out of Libby before she could stop them; goading her father would do no good, but the clench of his jaw gave her a millisecond of satisfaction.

"In case you've forgotten, I own this house. You live here practically rent-free. That means I will turn up whenever I damn well please."

The chilly tone of his voice rankled Libby. She hated that he could sound so emotionless when talking to her. But that was exactly the point, her relationship with her father had never been about emotion. She was merely a trophy for his collection.

"I want you to leave." She would either scream or cry or hurl something at him if he didn't vanish from her sight in the next thirty seconds.

"I will leave when I am damn well ready."

"She wants you out of here." Paul walked through the entranceway into the living room, his face hard. "I suggest you do it."

Libby's breath caught in her throat. Having Paul here was going to make it worse. The last thing she wanted was for someone else to witness this humiliating exchange with her father. "How did you get in here?"

"The front door was unlocked. I heard yelling." He looked from Libby to her father and back again. His forehead creased, and his shoulders bunched around his neck as though he sensed the tension in the air and had embodied it.

"And you are?" Her father turned to Paul, his brow quirked in disdain.

"Libby's boyfriend." He folded his arms across his chest, unflinching in the face of Kirk Harris's legendary withering stare.

"Seems you've chosen your men as well as you've chosen your career," he said, looking back to Libby and shaking his head. "Why won't you let me help you?"

"Because you're not trying to help *me*." Her head swam, and she pressed her fingertips to her temples. "You're doing this for yourself."

"How can you say that?"

For a moment she wondered if there was a hint of emotion in his voice, a small crack in the tough outer shell that might allow her a peek inside. Did he really care about her deep down? She hated that even now a part of her still hoped it might be true.

"I don't want to talk about this, Dad. Please just go."

Paul took a step toward her father, his six-foot plus frame giving him an inch or two. Dressed all in black, he seemed even bigger. Stronger.

"Do I need to make you leave?" Paul asked. Unlike her father, his tone was filled with undisguised emotion.

Kirk tilted his chin. "I *own* this place."

"That doesn't give you the right to talk to Libby like that. Apologize to her and then leave." His dark eyes flashed like black fire.

"I will do as I please."

Paul grabbed her father by the shoulder. The grip wouldn't be enough to do any serious damage, but the message was clear. He leaned in close and whispered something that made the blood drain from her father's face.

When Paul released him, the older man glared at Libby before stalking toward the front door.

"You should start looking for somewhere new to live," her father said in his usual ice-cold tone just before the door slammed shut behind him.

"What did you say to him?" she asked, wariness spreading through her system and making her limbs heavy.

"I simply reminded him that as a father it's his job to take care of his daughter, not to treat her like a piece of meat."

"I'm sure you said it so eloquently as well."

Paul smirked. "I may have colored outside the lines a little."

She shoved her shaking hands into the pockets of her sundress. Having Paul witness the truth behind her family—especially after seeing how loving and caring his family was—made her feel exposed, like he could see the fabric of imperfections that she'd tried so hard to cover up.

She was unlovable, and it shamed her.

"I wish you didn't see that." She sucked on her top lip and turned away from him, needing a moment to gather herself.

"Why?"

She shrugged, unable to speak past the lump in her throat. Heat burned in her chest and neck. She walked to the fridge, her heels clicking against the tiled floor, and reached for a bottle of water.

So much for keeping Paul at a distance. The image of him standing there—protecting her, defending her—rolled around in her brain. No one had ever done that for her before…and it felt good.

The guy's clearly a jerk. It's not a reflection of you."

Libby didn't turn around, so Paul had full view of her copper hair as it tumbled down the back of the white dress she wore. The sharp contrast struck a chord in him; she looked like a painting. Unreal.

Perfect.

Except that her guard had shot up the minute he walked in the front door. No surprise there, her father was a Grade A prick. If it had been anyone else they'd be sporting a broken nose for talking to her in such a demeaning way.

Getting him out of the house before he caused the guy some serious damage had been tough.

Tightness gripped his chest. She wasn't his to protect, in reality, she wasn't *his* at all. So why did he feel that roar of desire to pull her into his arms and comfort her? He did *not* comfort women.

That was a job for real boyfriends.

But the question hovered on his tongue, needling at him. "Are you okay?"

She nodded. "You're right. He's a total jerk...sadly, I'm used to it."

"So this isn't just because you've dropped out of med school?"

"No, it's not. He treated my mother like crap for as long as I can remember." She turned and closed the fridge, leaning back against it while she sipped water from a bottle. "They only got married because she got pregnant at nineteen. They fought most of the time while I was growing up, and they ended up divorcing when I was ten."

He listened as her history tumbled from her mouth in a rush of words as if she'd been trying to get it out for a long time. Normally this would be his idea of hell—being a shoulder to cry on wasn't exactly his forte outside the sob stories he occasionally got at the bar.

But he found himself wanting to listen to Libby, wanting to be the person she turned to...not that he had even the slightest clue as to what to say to her in return. He'd always been better with actions than words.

"Mum got nothing out of the divorce. Dad had made her sign a prenup, and she ended up working crazy hours to make rent in the area where I went to school. Dad paid for my education, but he made it hard for her whenever he could. I think by the time she remarried and had another kid she didn't want to see me much because I reminded her of all that."

"And your Dad remarried?"

"He's onto his *fourth* wife. It's no wonder I don't believe in marriage." She rolled her eyes.

Paul let out a long, low whistle. "Fourth? At some point you just have to admit that something's not working."

"I swear, each one gets worse than the last. It's like he purposefully tries to find these vapid, gold-digging wenches without a brain in their head. This current one could be on one of those *Real Housewives* TV shows."

Paul cringed.

"My mother wasn't like that, but she has a new family now." The sadness in her voice hit him like a punch to the solar plexus. "I'm sorry, I don't know why I'm telling you all this. You're probably bored to tears."

"Not even a little bit," he said, motioning for her to continue.

She picked at the hem of her dress, her brows burrowed into a deep frown. "Dad's good at forcing people to do what he wants. It's one of the reasons I want to make this business work. If I make my own money I can do what I like. I never really wanted to be a doctor."

"What did you want to be?"

"You know, I have no idea. I poured so much energy into trying to please him I never thought about what I actually wanted. Then by the time I decided I wanted to do my own thing I had no idea which direction to take."

"It's not too late, you're still young."

"So are you," she pointed out.

He shrugged. "I'll be fine so long as I can get the family off my back."

"They don't seem that bad."

"It's more the extended family. They're old school, they think anyone who doesn't have a degree or some form of qualification is going to be a loser their whole life." He leaned back against the couch, reducing the space between them. "I don't care, I do what I like."

"Obviously you *do* care, since I'm playing the role of happy girlfriend." She paused. "Unless there's more to the situation than you're telling me."

"I'm helping you out."

She grinned, like a cat who'd caught the scent of a mouse. "Nah, there needs to be something in it for you. It's not just judgment from your family, is it? Who's going to be at the wedding that you're so worried about?"

He clenched his teeth, his jaw tightening until the muscles ached. "I don't want to talk about it."

"Okay." She held up her hands in retreat. "I just thought since I poured my heart out to you that you might want to reciprocate."

"There's no point talking about it. It doesn't change the situation." He needed to change the topic, stat. "Actually, I had an idea that I wanted to discuss with you."

She raised a brow. "Sure."

"I want to start up my own mixology school at First."

He sucked in a breath, annoyed at how nervous he was about sharing it with Libby. The idea had come to him like a bolt of lightning when one of the new waitresses had asked him to show her how to make a cosmopolitan. He suspected the request was a ploy to talk to him, but after he'd started teaching her about the proper way to mix cocktails she'd seemed genuinely excited to try it on her own.

"We could run classes on how to create professional cocktails at home or for parties, teach people the theory behind mixing the perfect drink. Since you're trying to get your product in there, we could pitch it as a branding partnership." He tried to keep his face neutral, but waiting for her reaction was killing him.

"I love it!" She clapped her hands together and laughed. "It's perfect. It will make my product look more attractive, and I could include some promotional gifts as an incentive to customers…and Des."

The genuine excitement on her face made his blood rush. Ideas for how they could pitch the mixology school to his brother came tumbling out, their energy and creativity matched. Eventually, when the well ran dry, Libby motioned for him to follow her into the living room.

"By the way, I wanted to say thanks for getting my dad out of here earlier. Whatever you said seemed to have worked, but you don't have to play white knight."

"It's nothing. I've been the bouncer at First on more than one occasion." He shrugged it off, but deep down her thanks warmed him.

"Oh yeah?" She smiled, the white dress swishing around her knees as she walked.

The straps were like two thin strands of spaghetti, leaving most of her shoulders and chest bare. A hint of cleavage tempted him, the creamy expanse of her skin dotted with a few freckles. He wanted to connect them by drawing lines with his tongue.

"I've kicked out a fair share of drunks, broke up a few fights. It can get a little crazy on a Friday night."

"But there must be perks…I bet you have your pick of the ladies." She dropped down onto the sofa and kicked off her heels, crossing her legs demurely.

"Why? Do you think I'm hot?" he teased.

Her cheeks flushed, and she tried to cover it by pressing her water bottle to her neck. The air hung heavy with summer heat, despite the churn of an air conditioning unit overhead. Condensation from the bottle dripped onto her skin. A lone droplet ran down the length of her neck and made a beeline for the sweet valley between her breasts.

"No comment," she said, fanning herself.

He took the spot next to her on the couch. "So you felt absolutely nothing when you kissed me?"

"*You* kissed *me*." She gestured with her water bottle. "I was happy to play the polite, conservative girlfriend."

"They would never have bought it. I don't go for conservative types."

"So you prefer med school dropouts with a penchant for expensive shoes?" She lifted her hair from her neck and wound it into a knot on top of her head.

"That's quite a niche." He tilted his head, watching her closely. "There hasn't really been anyone in a while, to be honest."

"How come?"

He shrugged, pushing his fingers through the inky black curls on his head. "I don't want to be in a relationship, but the dating scene got old. Too many games for me."

Nodding, she secured her hair with a hair band from her pocket. Wispy sections escaped around her face, framing those sharp hazel eyes and her perfectly pale skin. "I know what you mean. I haven't dated anyone in…forever. But I didn't really like the idea of constantly jumping from one guy to another, so I stopped altogether."

"Relationships aren't a very good alternative, though."

"I can see why so many people do the friends with

benefits thing. You just take a good personal connection and add sex, but there's no emotion. No messy stuff."

"There's *some* messy stuff." He chuckled and she rolled her eyes.

"You're such a guy."

"I try."

"So are you going to find a new place?"

She looked as though she might call him on turning the tables on her, but she didn't. "I should but that would require me to be making some money of my own. I sank a lot of what I had into the business. I didn't want to be saddled with a loan so I used my savings. I don't have enough for a deposit on a new place."

"I will do everything I can to make sure you get into First and get your business off the ground." The words slipped out before he could think to stop them. "You know, since that's what a boyfriend would do."

"I appreciate that. But you know you don't have to play boyfriend if we don't have an audience, right?"

"Why? Don't think you can handle me if it's just the two of us?"

She shifted on the spot. "I didn't say that."

"Are you worried you wouldn't be able to say no to me?" A surge of desire flooded him as she blinked, her cheeks flushed. "Just like you melted into a puddle when I kissed you."

"I *can* say no to you, Mr. Cocky." She jabbed a finger into his chest. "You're not God's gift to women, you know."

"I've been told things to the contrary." He grinned, enjoying putting her on the spot. It was like the adult equivalent of tugging her pigtails.

"You're far more tempted by me than I am by you." She shoved her chin up into the air and looked him square in the eye.

"Is that so?" God damn if he didn't love a challenge.

"Yep." She nodded, spurred on by her own false bravado. "You came up with the excuse to kiss me in the kitchen, and you're the one who turned up today out of the blue."

"You say that like you haven't been debating whether to call me all week."

"I haven't." She blinked rapidly.

"I'm sorry, you'll need to start speaking English again. I don't understand bullshit."

Her mouth formed a shocked *O*, and she shoved him in the shoulder. "You're so unbelievably cocky."

"You love it."

"I definitely do *not*."

An impulse shot through him, the desire to do something totally wrong and stupid and oh-so-worth-it. "We're going to settle this with a game of chicken."

"Chicken?"

He nodded, raking his eyes over her so she knew *exactly* how much trouble she was in. "I'm going to kiss you for a whole minute, and you're going to tell me to stop when the timer goes off."

She raised a brow. "You can't be serious."

"I'm one hundred percent serious." He pulled the phone out of his pocket and opened up the stopwatch app. "One minute. Then you can put me in my place."

"No way."

"Think you're going to lose?"

Her hazel eyes sparked. If there was one thing he'd

learned—and deeply enjoyed—about Libby, it was her competitive streak.

She took a swig of her water bottle as if she didn't have a care in the world. "I never lose."

"Then you've got one minute." He set the phone on the table and purposely didn't switch on the timer.

But before Libby noticed, he turned to her and cupped her sweet face with both his hands. He made her look at him—*really* look at him—before he brought his mouth down to hers. Her breath hitched at the light kiss he planted on the corner of her mouth, at the gentle swipe of his tongue as he taunted himself with the barest taste of her.

Going slow seemed impossible when his whole body screamed *more, more, more*.

"I'm not even a little bit tempted," she whispered, though her eyes fluttered closed the second his lips came back to hers.

"Bullshit."

He captured her mouth, opening her up like a flower under the first beam of summer sunlight. Her lips were cool from the water bottle, but her mouth was hot. Thrusting his hands into her hair, he pulled her head back with a swift tug, exposing her neck. Floral perfume mingled with the scent of soap and skin.

He trailed a line from her jaw to the base of her neck, feeling her pulse flutter wildly beneath his touch.

"You're a terrible kisser." Her words came out raspy, broken.

Terrible? He brought his mouth back to hers and punished her for the lie. The sensation of her tongue against his made him so hard he might never recover, not till he satiated himself deep inside her. God, he wanted her. Every time he saw her that want grew, expanding and consuming the areas of his mind that should be used for other things.

Like motor skills. And breathing.

She moaned, the raw sound of pleasure setting off every alarm bell in his head. But there would be no stopping him unless she called for an end. Which she wouldn't, of that he was certain.

The bare skin of her shoulders and chest tempted him. All the creamy, smooth porcelain in contrast to the rich tan of his hands. Like they were made to complement each other. He moved down to the base of her neck, tracing the line of it with his thumb. "Still think it's terrible?" he asked, the gentle curve of her breast filling his palm. His thumb caught a hardened nipple, rolling it gently as he nipped on her lower lip. The light fabric of her dress couldn't conceal the life radiating from her like heat shimmering off smoldering tar.

The ache for her built; with each breathy little moan his need grew. *He* grew.

Her tongue clashed with his, her back arching to increase the friction between them so he slid his arm around her waist and pulled her down until she was beneath him. He pressed her into the couch, the sweet heat from her parted legs making his blood fizz and hiss.

"Paul," she gasped, as he pressed his cock against her. "We agreed…"

"What?" He fought the urge to tear off her underwear and plunge deep inside her. This was his game, he had to maintain a modicum of control. But it dangled by a thread, her sweet hands digging into his back. Pressing him against her.

Pushing his limits.

"No sex." The words trailed off into a soft moan.

"This isn't sex." Burying his face into her neck, he nipped at the smooth flesh there while his hands pushed her dress up. "We're just kissing."

"It's more than that."

Under the frothy layers his hands found her, damp and hot. He pressed the heel of his hand to her center, his insides roaring as she ground against him. Libby was so sweetly responsive, so sensual.

So unbelievably sexy.

"Oh Paul, it's…" She bucked her hips as he hooked a finger inside her underwear. "This is a terrible idea."

But as he stroked her slowly, feeling her desire as she trembled beneath him, she pressed against his hand. He'd barely touched her and already she was close. Cool air hit his skin as she pushed his T-shirt up, her nails scraping along his chest.

"That's got to be longer than a minute." She clamped her teeth down on her bottom lip as he slid a finger into her.

Heat radiated from her. The muscles of her sex clenched around him, urging him on. Drawing him deeper.

"Do you want me to stop?"

"You better not." Her eyes clamped shut, a moan escaping her mouth.

Pink flashed as her tongue darted out to moisten her lips, and he captured it. Sucking on it as he stroked her.

He pressed his thumb to her clit, the tight bundle of nerves swollen and needy. Another tremor ran through her. She rolled her hips, trying to take control of the rhythm. But he was in charge here — for now she'd have to follow his lead.

His touch.

Clenching his bicep, she rocked against his hand. He'd have the mark of her nails in his skin soon, and that knowledge made his cock swell to bursting point. But he wouldn't deny her, not when she was so close.

No matter how desperate he was to feel her shatter while he was inside her.

"Please."

"What do you need?" He drank her in, slipping a second finger inside her and feeling the muscles tighten.

"I need…" she gasped. "Paul, make me come."

He dropped his head beneath her skirts and shoved her underwear aside. The sound of delicate fabric ripping cut through the air but nothing mattered except getting his mouth on her. His lips barely touched her before she shook, a sharp cry echoing through the house as she came.

Watching Libby orgasm was the most gratifying thing he'd ever experienced. As she released her grip on his hair her eyes fluttered open, a smile curved on her luscious lips. She opened her mouth to speak when a sudden knock at the door shattered the mood.

Chapter Seven

There were bad life decisions, like bleaching your hair to within an inch of its life. Then there were the kind of decisions that were not only colossally stupid, but had immediate ramifications. Like letting your fake boyfriend give you a "dare orgasm" while someone knocked at your front door.

Libby resisted the urge to curl into a ball. The last waves of her climax still washed through her, though Paul had withdrawn his hand and—thankfully—returned her dress to its rightful place.

The knocking sounded again. She'd recognize the owner of that knock anywhere: three sharp raps that weren't melodic or careless in any way. Nina.

"Should I hide in a cupboard?" Paul looked at her with a wicked glint in his eye.

"It's fine, just…" Libby pushed up from the couch and tried to fix her appearance. "Act cool."

He laughed. "Says you."

She caught her reflection on the way to the door. Pink cheeks, a rumpled dress, and disheveled hair…she may as well hang a sign around her neck that said, "Hey, I just had an orgasm. It was great!"

As she opened the door, Nina burst forth. "I thought I was going to have to send a search squad. You've been avoiding me. What the hell is going—"

The words died on her lips as she took in Libby's appearance. Her eyes moved to Paul, who made his way across the room in a lazy swagger that spelled sex and sinfulness. His hair, mussed by her fingers, had that slept-in look to it. Libby gulped.

Oh crap! Nina is going to kill me. No matter which way I spin it, she's going to know I've kept her in the dark.

Nina looked at Libby pointedly, awaiting an introduction. The words stuck in Libby's throat. Should she introduce him as her boyfriend and thereby continue the lie? Or should she come clean and wear Nina's judgment?

"I'm Paul," he said, sticking out his hand—the one that didn't bring her to orgasm—and offering a charming smile.

"Nina." She looked at him closely. "You're the guy from the bar, aren't you? You were there when Libby sprained her ankle."

"Yes, I'm the bar manager at First. We're interested in Libby's business, so she was kind enough to talk me through how she makes her product."

"Oh." Nina nodded, some of the suspicion seeping out of her features. "That's great."

"Nina is the one responsible for all the artwork I showed you." Libby looked up at Paul, hoping to hell her features didn't betray her.

Cool as a cucumber, you can do it!

"You make a great team." He looked at his phone and shoved it into his back pocket. "I should be heading off."

"Meet me in the office, Neens. I just need to finish up with Paul." Libby swallowed the giggle that bubbled up in her throat.

Maybe it was the fact that she'd had her first orgasm in months—one that didn't come from her own hand—or perhaps it was just that she was doing something naughty for once, but Libby felt giddy with the danger of it all. She never lied to her friends, and it had been an age since she got involved with a guy for anything more than scratching an itch.

But she had to remember that's all it was, a silly mistake. Paul was just the kind of guy to have a girl melting at his feet, that's why he was so damn good at it! She had to stay away; getting involved with a ladies' man was not on her agenda.

"Nice to meet you, Paul." Nina nodded and retreated into the depths of the house.

"Outside. Now." Paul's breath tickled her ear as the whispered command sent a shiver down her spine.

"Did you even set the timer?" she asked as they walked out onto the front of the house. She closed the door behind her.

"You seemed so certain that you'd be able to say no, I didn't think you needed it." He looked so smug she wanted to kick him in the shins and wipe that self-satisfied grin off his face.

"I'll get you back, you know that, right?"

"I look forward to it, Tiger." He leaned in and pressed his lips to her cheek. "See you later."

He made it halfway down the driveway before Libby

found her voice. "Why did you come by today, anyway?"

"I wanted to tell you about the mixology idea…and Gracie and Des are coming for dinner tomorrow night. Bring some of your product around and we'll give them a chance to try it firsthand. I'll text you the details."

"You could have just called." She planted her hands on her hips.

"Aren't you glad I didn't?"

Without waiting for her to respond, he headed toward his car with the kind of hip-rolling gait that was hot enough to singe a girl's panties. Speaking of panties, hers were… irreparable.

Libby waited until Paul had driven off before she headed back into the house, undoubtedly to face an inquisition from Nina. Paul had covered when words failed her, but her best friend wasn't so easily fooled.

She found Nina sitting on her desk, twirling a strand of her bright blue hair around one finger.

"Spill," she demanded.

"Spill what?" Libby shrugged innocently and went to her stock cabinet to select a few bottles to present to Des and Gracie.

"You don't expect me to believe that gorgeous hunk of a man was here purely for business." She raised a brow. "Or did you get that JBF look all by yourself?"

"JBF?"

"Just been fucked."

Libby held up a hand in surrender. "So we kissed, no big deal."

"You did more than kiss."

Libby sighed and plucked out a bottle of lemon myrtle

vodka. "Why would you think that?"

"Oh, I don't know." Nina shrugged. "Maybe because you've got that puppy-dog look on your face. Or maybe because his jeans were more revealing than he probably wanted them to be."

Heat surged through Libby, the memory of Paul's hands on her fresh and raw. It was lucky that Nina had interrupted them—she would have given him anything at that point. At least now she had a minor indiscretion on her record rather than a full-blown fake relationship violation.

"Lucky you, by the way, and you're a *terrible* liar." Nina winked in her usual lewd manner and burst out laughing when Libby looked at her guiltily. "Did you sleep with him?"

"No," she sighed. "But I was damn close."

"You should have put a bloody sock on the door or something. I don't want to be the source of your continued sexual frustration."

"I'm not the one who's frustrated." She couldn't stifle her grin.

"You dirty birdy!" Nina slapped her palm down on the surface of the table. "I love it."

"So did I, unfortunately," Libby muttered.

Tomorrow night she'd have to keep her cool. She may have slipped up, but that wasn't a reason to throw it all in. Paul was dangerous, and she'd already opened up to him more about her past than any other person with the exception of Nina. She didn't want a relationship, and talking about personal stuff before sex was definitely relationship territory.

She had to put a stop to it now, no matter how much she wanted to return the favor.

Since meeting Libby, Paul found himself uninterested in other women. Temptation hadn't once caught his eye at the bar or anywhere else. All he could think of was the plucky redhead who'd burst into his life and not only given him a permanent hard-on, but had made him feel things that had been locked away for a long time.

Like possessiveness. The need to protect. A desire to listen and learn.

These were all things he hadn't experienced since Sadie, but the comparison terrified him. They were very different people, but some of the traits that had pulled him and Sadie apart were the things that attracted him to Libby, like her ambition. That wonderful competitive streak. Her relentless pursuit of what she wanted. Those similarities were so clear, in fact, that he could see the way their future would unfold… right down to the exact scene where she was packing her bags and leaving him.

He couldn't let her get under his skin.

Focusing on the fact that Libby drove him crazy with her passion, despite trying her hardest to hide it, would be the best thing he could do. After leaving her house yesterday he'd had the mother of all cold showers, but the memory of her splayed out on that couch would not abate.

Now he was trying to cook something that didn't resemble prison food, all so they could have another opportunity to pitch her product and the mixology school to Des.

He raked a hand through his hair. At least it had distracted him from the black cloud that was Des and Gracie's wedding. Although if he was being honest with himself, being needed by someone like Libby made him feel alive…not that any amount of water torture would force him to admit those words aloud.

It's just pent-up sexual frustration; you don't really feel anything for her. Remember what she said, it's just business.

Or had they crossed that line when she told him about her family? Was that her way of leaving things open enough for him to want more?

The doorbell buzzed, pulling Paul away from his thoughts.

"Hey," he said, holding the door open for Libby. "Give me that box, it looks heavy."

"I can manage." She offered a stiff smile and tried to shuffle past, but he held out an arm, and she begrudgingly placed the box there.

"What the hell did you pack in here? Bricks?" He balanced it on one side and shut the door with his free hand.

"Lots and lots and lots of vodka."

"Perfect." He grinned.

Libby dropped her bag and a folder onto his couch, her eyes darting around the room. Her hands fidgeted with her hair, which had been piled on top of her head. Agitation marred her normally graceful movement.

"Are you nervous?" he asked, setting the box down on top of the coffee table so he could unpack it.

"A little," she admitted, without meeting his gaze. "I think it's because I know he's rejected me once already."

"So?"

"I'm manipulating him. *We're* manipulating him." She dropped down on the couch and knotted her hands in her lap. "Don't you feel bad about that?"

Yeah, he did. More than he wanted to. But somehow the knowledge that he was helping Libby seemed to override everything else. Besides, Des hadn't really given her a fair chance. Tonight Libby's hard work and his ideas would do the talking.

"What would be the difference if we were really dating?" he asked. "And I thought you said you'd do anything to make your business a success."

He pulled out six bottles of vodka in a variety of flavors. Each had its own colored label sporting the Libby Gal logo. They looked feminine and professional, something he could easily imagine selling out at First. Des had been a fool not to see that.

"Why don't we make them a cocktail?" he said, carrying the bottles to his bar.

The bar was the area in his house where he felt most comfortable, the creative outlet he craved when everything else turned to shit. He'd built it himself, customized it to exactly what he wanted. The shelves were stocked with his favorite spirits and liquors, a bar fridge contained other ingredients required for cocktail creation, and a wine fridge sat next to it.

"Wow, this is amazing." Libby ran her hand along the bar's polished surface. "You've got everything here."

"What can I say, I like to drink." He shrugged.

"No, you like to *create*." Her eyes lit up, the anxiousness from earlier draining out of her features as she went behind the bar. "If you just liked to drink you'd have a fridge full of beer like every other man in Australia."

She turned to the rows of cocktail glasses hanging upside down beside tumblers, highballs, and shot glasses. Her fingertips danced along the stem of a martini glass.

"Which of those is your favorite?" He turned the vodka bottles so they all faced the same way like a rainbow of infused goodness. Lemon myrtle, marshmallow and rose petal, fig and vanilla bean, lavender, basil and orange, strawberry and spearmint.

"The marshmallow and rose petal." She picked up the bottle with the pink label. "I made this for a friend's wedding, and it's what gave me the confidence to start Libby Gal Cocktails."

He nodded and took the bottle from her, opening it. The scent of fluffy pink candies danced with delicate rose petals, it was definitely *not* the flavor Paul would have chosen but this was about Libby's tastes, not his.

He grabbed two shot glasses from the bar and filled them to the brim. "Drink."

"I thought we were supposed to be making cocktails for Gracie and Des." She took the shot glass and smirked at him.

"*Salute!*" He raised his shot glass.

"What does that mean?"

"To good health."

She nodded and clinked her glass against his. "*Salute.*"

They downed the vodka and Paul had to admit, as much as it tasted like something that could have been squeezed out of a unicorn, it was tasty. An idea took shape in his mind.

"Okay, so we're going to make a Bellini." He grabbed a bottle of Prosecco from the wine fridge. "Grab four of the champagne flutes."

Libby complied and lined them up in a neat row in front of him. "Bellinis don't have vodka, do they?"

"Not usually." He eased the cork out of the bottle with a

pop. "But I used to make Absolut Bellinis when I was living in London."

"You lived in London? I didn't know that." She watched him with curious eyes, her arms propped up on the bar's surface.

"Spent a year there in between some backpacking stretches. I wanted to see the world. That's how I started working behind a bar—it was the perfect job for me to party and get paid at the same time." He winked.

She shook her head, smiling as he measured out the vodka into each glass and then followed it with pureed cherries. As the Prosecco was added, the red puree swirled, coloring the wine and mixing in the vodka until the glass graduated from clear to hot pink.

"That looks amazing."

He placed a cherry in each glass. "Voilà."

"There's a story behind this, isn't there?" She breathed in the scent of the drink. "The cherry goes so well with the rose and marshmallow, why didn't I think of that?"

The way she looked up at Paul could have knocked him dead on the spot. The admiration shining out of that beautiful face made him want to sweep the drinks to the floor and take her right there on the spot.

"You'll have to ask Gracie about that story," he said, brushing his hands down the front of his jeans. "Want another sneaky shot before dinner?"

"I'll be under the table before the food comes out." She held up her hands and laughed. "Multiple shots on an empty stomach is a bad idea."

"I'm open to bad ideas," he said, stalking around the side of the bar and placing his hands on her shoulders.

She swallowed, her eyes darkening instantly. "That's why I need to be careful around you."

Paul opened his mouth to protest but Gracie's shrill giggle came from outside the house. Bad ideas would have to wait—tonight they were on a mission.

Chapter Eight

"These are seriously delicious," Gracie said, knocking back the remainder of her third cherry vodka Bellini. "And they smell amazing. What flavor is the vodka again?"

"This one is marshmallow and rose." Libby jumped up from the table and brought the bottle over. "It's my personal favorite."

Gracie unscrewed the cap and took in a big breath. "I love it, and I adore this cocktail. I would never have thought to put the cherry *in* the Bellini."

"I'm curious, what's the story behind it?" Libby asked, taking a long sip of her cocktail.

At the current rate, Gracie was drinking her under the table. Libby was halfway through her second drink, and Gracie was motioning for Paul to make her number four.

"Didn't Paul tell you?"

Libby shook her head and watched as Paul mixed another drink. His shirtsleeves had been rolled up, revealing strong forearms covered in a smattering of dark hair. His eyes caught hers, crinkling as he stifled a smile.

Busted.

"Oh, it's such a funny story." Gracie grabbed Des's hand and gave it a squeeze. "I used to bring all these loser guys to First because I had it stuck in my head that I needed to marry some corporate bigwig. But they were always terrible! When I ordered a Bellini with a cherry on the side that was Des's signal to come and save me."

"It took her a while to figure out I was the better choice," Des said with exaggerated smugness, though his love for Gracie filled the room like a heady perfume.

Libby's heart squeezed. She had no idea how it felt to be looked at as though you were the only thing in the world that mattered. But she'd bet her last dollar it would make everything else pale in comparison.

"But I got there in the end, didn't I?" Gracie beamed, her eyes bright, cheeks pink with love and alcohol.

"You sure did."

"That's such a lovely story." Libby didn't try to hide the awe and envy in her voice. If Paul questioned her she'd claim to be an amazing actress. Again.

"So you came up with all these vodka recipes yourself?" Des asked.

The boys had moved on from the cocktails to straight shots after dinner had been cleared away. Now they all sat around the table, feasting on a bowl of chocolates that Libby brought with her and sampling the vodka flavors.

"I started out following recipes I found online." Libby selected a chocolate with a bright green foil wrapper. "But then I experimented with my own. These six flavors are the core ones I decided to launch up front, but I'm currently perfecting another four flavors and I'm in early stages of testing a few others."

"I like the orange and basil," Des said, lifting the bottle to his nose. "It's not sweet at all."

"It works really well as a mixer with plain soda water or tonic water. I felt like I needed something a little more masculine given how sweet some of the other flavors are."

Des nodded. "I'll be honest, when you first came to me I thought the whole thing was a bit gimmicky. But I misjudged the product—it's really good."

Hope curled in Libby's gut; she had the feeling Des wasn't one to hand out praise too easily. This was definitely a positive step forward, all she had to do now was convince him that his customers would select her bottles from the shelf.

"Having a few flavored vodkas would really open up the opportunity for a specialized cocktail menu," Paul interjected, opening the last bottle and pouring four shots. "And mixology classes."

Des raised a brow. "Mixology classes?"

"Libby and I came up with this brilliant idea—"

"I'm not taking credit," she said, holding up her hands. "That was all you."

"We—I—want to start up my own mixology school. I thought we could run classes on how to create professional cocktails at home or for parties, teach people the theory behind mixing the perfect drink. It would be a perfect branding partnership for Libby Gal Cocktails as well." His face was neutral but she sensed a nervous energy in the way he bounced his leg next to hers under the table. "I could run it during the week. It will bring more people into the bar on our quiet nights, make some extra revenue if we couple the classes with a dinner here."

"Do you have a business plan?" Des asked.

"Uh…no."

"A concept without a business plan is just an idea. I'd need to see numbers, stats, and how you think we'll fund this activity before I can even consider it."

Paul looked as though he'd run full speed into a brick wall. Sure, she hadn't expected Des to fawn over his idea, but some semblance of positive feedback would have been nice. Some brotherly support perhaps?

Knowing Des a little better, she had the feeling it wasn't personal. He took his business very seriously, and Paul was his younger brother. Maybe this had something to do with why Paul felt it necessary to have a fake girlfriend?

"Sure, I'll put something together," Paul said.

"I'm not going to be able to make it to the car if we keep drinking at this rate," Gracie said, in an obvious attempt to move the conversation along. However, she didn't hesitate to accept another shot when Paul handed it to her. "Is this lavender?"

"Yeah, I source it from a huge farm in Daylesford. They have a whole food and drink menu based around it, and that's where I got the idea to make a lavender infusion." She turned to Des. "You might like this one, too. I didn't add anything sweet to it, so it's more herbal than floral."

"Lavender?" He looked sceptical. "I guess we'll soon find out."

"*Salute!*" Paul lifted his glass, and everyone else followed.

Glasses slammed down against the table in a disjointed

beat. Libby's head swam with fuzzy warmth. She'd have to ease off if she had any chance of being able to drive home… ever. Frowning, she stole a glance at the clock. The hour hand hovered just before the ten. She'd definitely be getting a cab at this rate.

"You know," Gracie said, toying with her now empty shot glass. "The Bellinis would be a great thing to serve at the wedding. We could make them the toasting drink for the speeches."

"Wouldn't your mother have a heart attack if we deviated from the very carefully selected menu she presented us with?" Des asked, a cheeky glint in his eye.

Gracie shot him a look. "We don't have to serve them all night, but I love the story behind our drink. We can make it part of our speech and then get the waiters to hand them out. They are absolutely beautiful."

"I could make you some miniature bottles to give away as gifts for your guests or bridal party," Libby offered. "I did it for a friend, and they looked so adorable. We did custom labels with drawings of the bride and groom."

"We haven't figured out the bonbonnière yet." Gracie turned to Des. "I know you were keen to do that since it's such a big Italian tradition."

The discussion between Gracie and Des dissolved into a checklist of wedding preparation activities.

Paul leaned in close to Libby. "You totally sold Des. He looked damn impressed."

"You think so?" She turned her head. He sat so close that his heat enveloped her, awareness danced along her nerves, filling her body with a delicious hum.

"You nailed it." He pressed his lips to the shell of her

ear, a throaty chuckle reverberating against her neck when she shivered. "I, on the other hand, need a business plan."

"I could help you with that."

"I'd prefer it if you help me with something else." He trailed a fingertip down the length of her neck.

"Don't think you can get all handsy just because we've had a few drinks," she whispered, shooting him a look.

"Isn't that what a boyfriend does?" He grinned. "You seemed to enjoy it yesterday."

When it came to seduction Paul could run rings around her...with his eyes closed and both hands tied behind his back.

"I've got an idea," Gracie suddenly announced, her eyes twinkling with mischievousness. "Since we have all this vodka at our disposal, why don't we play a drinking game?"

"You're going to have a killer hangover tomorrow," Des warned, brushing a stray curl from her face.

"I'll be fine." She waved off his concerns. "I want to play Never Have I Ever."

Paul groaned. "I don't feel like condemning myself tonight."

"Okay, I *definitely* want to play now." Libby raised a brow.

If he wouldn't open up to her under normal circumstances, maybe he'd let a few things slip in a competitive situation. Their arrangement was supposed to be business, but pleasure had crept in, and curiosity had followed close behind.

"Fine," Paul said, bending down close to her again. "But I won't hold back."

She sucked in a breath, willing her heart to beat more slowly. "Bring it."

"Why don't we fix the ladies a drink?" Des motioned for Paul to follow him to the bar. "Make sure Gracie's is 90 percent soda water."

"I heard that!" Gracie pointed at her fiancé.

"She's a big girl, she can handle herself," Paul replied, winking at Gracie.

"You haven't seen her hungover. She gets so miserable." Des shook his head ruefully. "I hate seeing her like that."

"Awww, true love," Libby said, her tone teasing though envy coursed through her like poison.

Since when did she want that? She shook her head, trying to dislodge the strange sensation. Instead she concentrated on watching Paul make their drinks, mesmerized by how his hands seemed to caress everything he touched. Or was she drunk?

Paul reached for some fresh tumblers and measured out half shots of vodka into each of the girl's glasses. He topped them up with plenty of soda water and added a dash of syrup.

At the rate her head was turning fuzzy, the watered-down drink would be a blessing.

"It's for their own good." Des slapped Paul on the back and returned to the table. "Can I get a reminder on the rules?"

"We go around in a circle and make a statement starting with never have I ever," Gracie said, accepting her drink from Paul. "If you've done the action then you take a drink. For example, if I say never have I ever gotten a tattoo, Des would have to drink but I wouldn't. Got it?"

"Let's go." Des reached for his own drink.

"I'll start," Libby volunteered, looking around the table

with a dramatic pause. "Never have I ever cheated on a test."

Both Chapman boys took a swig of their drinks and looked at each other, laughing. Seeing them together in such a relaxed atmosphere, they were startlingly alike: dark hair, darker eyes, olive skin, and great bodies. But Paul had a mischievous charm about him whereas Des was more serious, the typical older brother.

"Delinquents." Gracie shook her head. "Never have I ever been to Europe."

The rest of the group all raised their glasses with a cheer and Gracie pouted.

"Never have I ever flashed someone," Paul said with a sly grin.

Silence settled over the table and curious eyes darted around the table until Libby took a swig of her drink. Her cheeks felt hotter than the pavement on a summer's day.

"I did Mardi Gras for my twenty-first birthday, so sue me."

"You wanted those beads, didn't you?" Paul threw back his head and laughed.

"Someone dared me, and you know how I am with dares."

His eyes darkened. "That I do."

"Never have I ever woken up somewhere and had no idea where I was." Des raised his glass but no one drank. "Nice to see we're all responsible adults here."

"Never have I ever dumped someone via text message." Libby looked around and Gracie took a swig of her own drink.

Paul followed. "Guilty as charged."

"That's terrible, guys," Libby admonished. "Don't you

think people deserve to have it said to their face?"

"The face-to-face breakup is overrated." Paul's lips twisted into a grimace, and Gracie nodded.

"I agree. Sometimes if you know the person is going to have a meltdown, text is better."

"You better not do that to me." Des pulled her into a hug and kissed the top of her head.

"Never," Gracie said solemnly. "Okay, never have I ever been publicly dumped."

Libby looked at her glass, contemplating a white lie. Paul would no doubt ask about it, and she hadn't really shared anything about her past relationships. Make that relationship. Singular. After that disaster she'd never gotten close to anyone…what was the point? Her ex had only reinforced what her parents taught her—relationships were risky, especially with men who had a lot of female attention, and there was little chance of reward.

"Define publicly?" Paul toyed with his glass. "Are we talking in front of a crowd?"

Gracie drummed her fingers on the tabletop. "In front of at least one person who wasn't in the relationship."

Paul picked up his glass and took a longer than necessary swig, looking at Libby the whole time as if daring her to ask him about it. His eyes remained hard, his jaw set tight. So he knew what it was like? No wonder a fake relationship appealed to him.

She responded in the only way she could, raising her glass and matching his gulp with hers.

"Aww, you poor things," Gracie said, crestfallen. "I was hoping no one would drink to that."

"Life goes on." Paul shrugged. "It won't happen to me

again, I'll make damn sure of that."

Libby reached out under the table and grabbed Paul's hand. She had no words, nothing that would soothe the past for either of them. Screw her ex and his, too. They were great people who deserved better than to be treated like garbage.

"Never have I ever had a nickname," Des said, breaking the tension and moving the game along.

When Libby didn't drink, Paul's elbow dug into her ribcage. "Why aren't you drinking?"

"I don't have a nickname," she said.

Gracie looked at her incredulous. "Never?"

"It's a lie," Paul brought the drink to her lips and held it there. "Your nickname is Tiger, in case you've forgotten."

He proceeded to stare at her until she took a sip of the drink, knowing she'd later regret accepting his declaration while he regaled the group with the story of how he came to give her the only nickname she'd ever had.

Glaring at him because she really did hate the nickname, she couldn't stop the spread of a smile across her lips. Nicknames and in-jokes weren't something she was used to. She'd never had any siblings to share them with, and her circle of close friends was shockingly limited.

For a moment she let herself believe that she belonged in Paul's world…no matter how dangerous she knew it to be.

When the drinking game had devolved into dirty questions that made the girls giggle, they all agreed to call it a night. Libby hugged Gracie, and they made plans to catch up and discuss the cocktails for the wedding.

"They're two peas in a pod, aren't they?" Des said, folding his arms across his chest. "She's good for you."

They stood at the front door, the summer breeze rolling in and carrying the scent of eucalyptus from the yard.

Paul raised a brow. "How so?"

"She's smart, fun. You're not chasing random tail at the bar anymore, you seem…focused. Happy."

"Yeah." He nodded.

Happiness wasn't something he'd ever worried much about before. He was an easygoing guy. Something that came from having low expectations. But he'd realized that there was a big difference between avoiding disappointment and being happy. Watching Libby kick goals tonight made his chest expand with pride. He was rooting for her, they were a team.

And that made him happy. The *real* kind of happy.

He said good-bye to Des and Gracie, his arm around Libby's waist. Her head rested against his chest, hair falling loose of its pins. As the door shut, she stepped out of his grip.

"I have to call a cab," she said, pressing her fingers to her temple. "There's no way I can drive like this."

"You're not catching a cab on your own." He shook his head. "Stay here."

She narrowed her eyes at him. "Nice try."

"I have a spare room, the bed's got fresh sheets and everything. You'll be comfortable." He gave her a pointed look. "And safe."

"I catch cabs by myself all the time." She collected the empty shot glasses and tumblers from the table and carried them to the kitchen.

"Don't tell me that." He followed with the remainder of

the bowls and glasses.

"And I don't want you getting any ideas." Her words were punctuated by the clatter of the plates being lowered into the sink.

He laughed. "Too late."

"You're terrible." She shook her head, but a smile twitched at the corner of her lips.

"I'm a guy, and you're the hottest woman to ever set foot in my house." He reached around her to place the glasses in the sink, his arms brushing her waist. "Plus, I don't like unfinished business."

"Unfinished business?" She blinked, her eyes wide as saucers.

He trapped her against the sink, and the memory of kissing her at his parents' house flooded him, chased by the vision of her beneath him. He was hard as a rock just thinking about it. Restless energy filled him with the need to touch, taste. Consume.

"You, me, your couch." His hands skimmed over her waist. "An untimely visitor."

She dropped her gaze, her hands coming up to his chest. God, he wanted those hands on him. He wanted that luscious, perfect mouth of hers on him. He wanted it all.

"So you got publicly dumped, too?" she asked, her cheek coming to rest on his chest.

If there was a quicker way for his libido to nosedive he couldn't think of it. "Why do you want to talk about that?"

"I want to know you, Paul. I get the feeling it's something that made an impact on you." The heat from her breath came in slow puffs through his shirt, tickling his skin.

He shielded himself against the memory. "I came home

and found her packing her things; she thought I was going to be out the whole day. Turns out she'd been cheating on me."

"And she admitted to it?"

"Yeah." He swallowed against the bitter taste in his mouth. "It was a bit hard for her to deny it when he was standing right there."

Her mouth dropped, and she looked at him with exactly the kind of pity he'd wanted to avoid. "Did you know the guy?"

I more than knew him; I'd spent every Christmas, birthday, and family event with him. He was my blood, my family.

"Yeah, I knew him." His muscles twitched.

Though he'd long stopped grieving the loss of both Sadie and his cousin, the hurt still kicked up from the bottom of his soul every so often like dirt at the bottom of a lake. He hadn't spoken to his cousin since that day, hadn't even uttered his name once.

"Do you want to hear my story?" She tilted her head.

Did he? Knowing her pain wouldn't make him feel any better, knowing that she understood didn't make a difference…did it? But chances were she hadn't asked to benefit him.

"Sure." He brushed a strand of hair out of her face and tucked it behind her ear, toying with her dangling earring for a moment. "Spill."

"I was sleeping with my TA at university." She let out a laugh, though her hazel eyes didn't crinkle as they normally did. "Not quite as cliché as sleeping with the professor, but close enough. I though he was the smartest, most brilliant man on the face of the earth."

"He couldn't have been that smart if he dumped you."

"He was smart when it came to manipulating people to get what he wanted. But then he was done with me, and I didn't take the hint. I tried calling him, texting him. When I approached him about why he was ignoring me, he told the coordinator that *I* came on to him and asked that I be removed from the class." She shook her head. "I had to explain my side of the story to the professor *and* the faculty coordinator. It was utterly humiliating, and in the end I gave up trying to get people to believe me. I was wrong about us getting serious, but I at least thought he respected me intellectually. Turns out he had female students lining up, and he'd chew them up and spit them out on a regular basis."

"So we're in agreement that relationships suck." He smoothed his hands over her shoulders and down the lengths of her arms. "What I don't understand is why you're punishing sex."

She laughed. "You're doggedly persistent, you know that, right?"

"It's not the worst thing I've been called by a long shot." He slipped his hands around her waist and dropped them down to her lower back, drawing her closer.

"I don't want anything to mess this up; we've got a good thing going here." She shrugged. "I'm making headway with Des and, if I can get my products into First, I'll have the proof of success all these other restaurants want. We'll get your mixology idea off the ground, and I'll do my bit by playing happy girlfriend at the wedding. We both walk away friends. No pain, no mess."

"Sex doesn't have to change that."

"What if you fall in love with me?" she teased.

"You're sexy as hell and smart to boot, but there ain't no

chance of that, Tiger."

He couldn't fall in love with her, no way, no how. Ambitious, well-to-do girls like Libby—and Sadie—wouldn't go the distance with him. They were always hungry for the next thing—they wanted more. And he couldn't give it to them. But what he could give them was the best damn sex of their lives.

A strange sensation twinged in his gut. This was exactly what had led him into an endless string of women warming his bed, and he was supposed to be done with that.

So why did Libby make him feel like it wasn't the empty kind of encounter he'd grown to hate?

She nodded, splaying her fingers flat against his chest. "Good."

"Is that a yes?"

"I don't believe you actually asked me a question."

He picked her up and set her on the edge of the kitchen bench, nudging her legs open so he could stand between them. The stretchy material of her polka dot skirt rode higher up over her thighs, revealing a flash of hot pink satin.

"I asked you to stay the night."

She waggled a finger at him. "You *told* me to stay."

"You want me to beg, Tiger?" He pressed his lips to the hollow at the base of her neck, his teeth scraping at her skin. "Not gonna happen. If anyone's going to beg, it'll be you."

Her head lolled back. "I don't beg."

"Oh you will." He kissed farther down, his hands deftly popping the buttons on her blouse. "I won't let you come until you beg shamelessly, incoherently. I'll hold you right on the edge until you say my name like it's the only word you know."

Her whole body trembled as his lips made it to the edge of her bra. Hot pink satin outlined with yellow lace, colorful and bold just like her. Hard nipples pressed against the fabric, drawing his eye and then his mouth. He tugged the cup down until he could taste all of her.

"Is that a yes?"

She sighed, her eyes fluttering closed. "You still haven't asked me."

"May I fuck you into oblivion?"

She laughed, her finger threading into his hair and yanking his face up. "Well, when you put it like that…"

"Say it."

"Yes, Paul." She brought her mouth to his in a hot open-mouthed kiss that set his whole body alight. "Yes."

Chapter Nine

Somehow they made it to his bed, though he was sure he'd find a trail of clothes leading like breadcrumbs to his kitchen in the morning. That was a problem for tomorrow, however, because he was certain about one thing—Libby wasn't leaving his bed until the sun came up.

Copper strands of hair fanned out across his pillow like silk streamers. She stared at him with hooded eyes, her hands reaching out.

"First things first, Tiger." He came down between her legs and blazed a trail with his mouth from belly button to the waistband of her single remaining item of clothing.

"Don't rip this pair," she said, her back arching as he pressed a kiss between her legs. "They're too pretty to go into the trash."

Pretty was an understatement. The swatch of pink silk against her pale, white skin was striking. Captivating.

It made him want to catalog every dirty thought he'd

ever had and play them all out at once.

"I'm impatient," he murmured against the silk before tugging the panties down her legs. "I don't want to waste a second."

He threw them to the side before capturing one ankle in his hand and hooking it around his waist.

"We have all night." She reached for his boxers, dipping her finger beneath the elastic to brush against his cock. The gentle scrape of her nails along his length dragged a moan from his lips.

He moved closer, allowing her to grasp him fully. "I'm going to need it. There's too many things I want to do to you."

Her tongue darted out to moisten her lips. "Are you sure I can keep up?"

"Don't worry about that. Let me drive," he said, pushing his boxers down and discarding them over the edge of the bed. "You just lie back and enjoy."

"Hmmm…" She wrapped her fingers around him and stroked slowly. "I like the sound of that."

His hands came down beside her as he lowered his face to hers, capturing her mouth in a deep, searching kiss. She tasted of marshmallow and chocolate, sweet. Decadent.

Through the haze of arousal and desperate desire, fear settled over him. Something felt different. Having Libby in his bed wasn't just about sex. It wasn't scratching an itch like he had in the past. He wanted to drown in her, he wanted to use his body to show her that she was beautiful, worthy. He wanted to erase her past hurts and make her feel whole.

"Correct me if I'm wrong, but you shouldn't be frowning during sex, right?" Her teeth nipped along his jaw, her tone teasing.

You got what you wanted, enjoy it. Don't think about anything beyond this. There isn't *anything beyond this.*

He bent his head and drew a nipple into his mouth, running his tongue over the tightened peak. Her moan echoed in the quiet room, awareness gripping him and quickening his pulse.

"I'm concentrating," he said, burying his face between her breasts. "I don't want you leaving until I've licked, kissed, and fucked every inch of you."

"You do have a way with words." She let out a throaty laugh as her head lolled back against the pillow and she arched against him. "Or maybe you're just good with your mouth."

"You should know the answer to that already."

A sly smile passed over her lips. "Refresh my memory?"

"Gladly."

He worked his way down to the juncture of her thighs, pressing kisses along the sensitive join of her hip. Warm flesh greeted his mouth. Goosebumps rippled across her skin as he trailed his fingertips over her thighs, skating around the part where she wanted him most. Her hips bucked as she fought for control, but Paul stayed true to his word.

"This is the part where you beg, Tiger."

He drew her clit into his mouth only to let it go a second later, lavishing maddening kisses all around her. One palm flattened against her stomach, holding her where he wanted her. Where she wouldn't be able to move without his permission.

"You can't make me," she panted.

"You're so close." He blew cold air over her sensitive

flesh, alternating direct pressure and feather-light licks. "It would be a shame not to hear that wonderful noise you make when you come."

"Paul," she growled.

"Yes, Tiger?"

Silence. She was stubborn, something he'd grown to appreciate. But he wanted her to know that in the bedroom she was at his mercy. This was his domain and if she bent then he would give her everything.

"Dammit." Her fist came down hard on the bed as she bucked her hips against his mouth.

"Say it."

"Please, I need it." She tangled her fingers in his hair and yanked him into place. "I'm begging."

"That's all you needed to say."

Her nails dug into his scalp as he applied the perfect pressure with his tongue, lapping at her until he tipped her over. The sound of her cries set his nervous system aflame. She trembled even after he drew his lips away, immediately curling into herself as the last shockwaves of orgasm ran through her.

He crawled up the bed and drew her to him, her back lining his front. Hot skin against hot skin. Wrapping his arms around her, his fingers traced the peaks and valleys of her beautiful body. He felt so…alive.

"It's not so bad to let someone else be in charge."

She turned, her face tilting up to his and catching the moonlight streaming in through the window. "Don't get cocky now."

He grinned. "Too late."

Shaking her head, she slipped out of his grasp and pushed

him back against the covers, straddling him. His hard-on brushed the creamy skin of her inner thigh. Wanting spread through him like a drug, heightening his senses, switching on the part of his brain that screamed *more, more, more.*

Rolling her hips in circles so that she bumped her heat against him, her eyes glittered. "Payback's going to feel so *very* good."

His fingers bit into her hips, his cock twitching with each brush of her satin skin. "Just because you're on top doesn't mean you're in the driver's seat."

He reached out to the drawer beside his bed and felt around for a condom. The foil crinkled as he ripped open the packet, cutting through the air heavy with arousal. He sheathed himself slowly, not missing the way Libby's eyes watched him intently.

"Do you like to watch?" He wrapped his hands around himself and stroked.

Pupils dilated, her breath hitched. Even in the dim light he could see the flush that crept across her cheeks, extending down her neck and matching the rosy shade of her nipples. Her hands curled into the bedspread as she watched, enraptured.

"I've never…" She swallowed. "I've never seen a man touch himself before."

The admission was fuel to his already out of control fire. He wanted to burst, but he controlled each stroke as though it were a master in resistance, power surging through him all the while.

"Do you like it?"

She licked her lips. "Very much."

"If I keep this up the show will be over before it's

begun." He released himself, reaching for her.

She came to him easily, her hips lifting to position over him. As she sank, a haze fell over him. His eyes rolled back, everything else fading away until it was just the sensation of her surrounding him.

"Paul," she gasped, her palms coming down on either side of his head.

"Easy, Tiger." He moved her hips to meet his thrusts, controlling the pace. Drawing out their pleasure.

Hair tickled his chest as her head rolled forward, the sheet of copper surrounding them until it felt as though they were the only two beings in the world. The pad of his thumb caught her lower lip as his hand curled around her jaw. She kissed the tip of his thumb, drawing him into her mouth and sucking in a way that made him want to combust.

"Keep that up…" he threatened.

"And what?" She blinked her long, black lashes at him. "You'll cross the finish line."

She squealed as he grabbed her hips, flipping them so that he hovered over her, still buried deep inside. Reaching down between them, he found the sensitive nub of her clit and started a slow assault. His favorite kind.

Her head pressed back into the pillow, eyes squeezed shut. "Oh my God—"

"I'm not going to cross the line until you scream my name again." He pressed a kiss to her mouth, catching her bottom lip between his teeth.

"You drive a hard bargain."

He chuckled against her throat, inhaling the scent of dampness on her skin mixed with faded perfume and soap. And something else…something uniquely her.

"It *is* hard."

She laughed, the sound dissolving into a cry as she reached the peak. He could have held back, but in that moment he wanted to give her everything: pleasure, completeness, satisfaction. He was at her service, there to command and form her pleasure.

"Paul," she whispered as the waves subsided. "Don't leave me out here alone."

"I won't." He thrust into her, driving toward the pinpoint of pleasure that blurred his vision and stole his breath. "I won't."

When orgasm hit he drowned in her. He didn't realize that he'd been calling her name until the rawness hit his throat, the echo of their lovemaking heavy in the air. Her arms wound around his waist, holding him against her.

For the first time in forever, having another's arms around him didn't feel like a trap.

Libby shifted, the haze of sleep slowly evaporating as she opened her eyes to the sunlight streaming through a window. A window with wooden slats and a distinct lack of color. In other words, not her window.

Head thumping, she tested the severity of her hangover by trying to lift her head from the pillow. Moderate, certainly not her worst, but she needed to down a painkiller and a bottle of water. Stat.

Heat prickled along her skin, the weight of Paul's arm heavy across her midsection. The bare skin of her back was fused to his chest, the backs of her thighs pressed against him.

What a night.

Heavy breathing told her he was still asleep...perhaps she could wriggle out and make a quick getaway to avoid the awkward morning-after chitchat. *Would* it be awkward? They had no expectations of each other, and they weren't in a relationship. They both shunned emotional entanglements.

Last night was nothing more than two people with mutual attraction blowing off a little steam. Or a lot of steam, as the case may be. For a moment she wondered how many women had woken up in his bed.

None of your business, don't even think about going there with him.

Aching limbs and niggling thoughts aside, Libby felt like a million bucks. Clearly all she'd needed to lessen the weight on her shoulders was a good, old-fashioned romp between the sheets. And too many orgasms to count. Paul was relentless, pushing her harder and higher each time until her body had nothing left to give.

"What was that little shiver for?" His sleepy voice sounded in her ear, his lips brushing the back of her neck.

"I think you're dreaming."

"Feels like it." He brushed his lips along the ridge of her shoulder. "I don't ever have a beautiful woman in my bed when I wake up in real life."

"Do you kick them all out before the sun comes up?" She rolled onto her back so she could see his face.

A hard mask settled over him, his eyes cold. "Something like that."

"I don't expect you to make me pancakes." Her hand came up to trace the hard line of his jaw. "Just so we're clear."

"So I should put the milk and eggs away?"

"You don't fool me, Paul Chapman. I know exactly what you want, and it's not breakfast."

He leaned over her, locking her down with his thigh and capturing her mouth with his. "You read me like a book."

"Right now you sound a lot like a teenage boy's diary. Sex on the brain."

He pretended to be hurt. "What else am I supposed to think about when you're lying there all naked and perfect like that?"

A warmth kindled in her chest. "My sparkling personality?"

"Not going to happen." His fingertips traced the length of her throat, his thumb skirting over the hollow at its base.

"What about how I'm a sharp business woman?" Her eyes fluttered shut as his hand trailed down to cup her breast.

"Tiger, all of those things are wonderful. But right now the only thing I want is to taste that sweet honey of yours."

Her sex clenched, but she resisted the urge to give in to him. "I really should go. I've got a lot of planning to do for the wedding."

His hand dipped lower, a flat palm smoothing over her belly to cup the gentle ache between her thighs. "What if I'm not done with you yet?"

"The best thing about sex without emotions is that I don't have worry about hurting your feelings." She sucked in a breath as he traced a line up her inner thigh.

"No, you just have to worry about your own." A dark shadow passed over his face, his eyes intently burning into her.

Something about the look unnerved her, as though she were crossing into new territory and wandering in the wrong direction. That was the problem with Paul, he drew her to him like a magnet. She knew she should leave his bed, she had work to do and an exciting opportunity in front of her.

But nothing else seemed to matter when he touched her.

Her worries about her business, about her father…everything melted away. But she didn't belong here with him. Her focus *had* to be on her business if she had any chance of making her own money and getting her own place. If she had any chance of being successful.

Not to mention that this relationship was fake because she could never be with someone like him…perfectly charming and sexy as hell. She wouldn't put herself in a situation where she had to compete for his attention. Been there, done that.

Never. Doing. It. Again.

"You know you've stopped telling me not to call you Tiger." His lips curved into a smile. "Does that mean I'm getting to you?"

"Or I've just realized that your persistence knows no bounds."

Deep down, in some dark corner of herself that she'd deny until the end of time, she'd grown to like it. A nickname signaled belonging, affection. Things she'd been hard up for most of her life, and he'd given them to her even when her reaction was to keep him at a distance.

"You don't get anywhere in life without persistence."

"Wise words." She kissed the tip of his nose. "But I do have to go. We're going to kill it at the wedding, you know. My cocktails will wow everyone, and I'm going to convince the whole family that you're perfect husband material."

"Let's not get carried away." He wrinkled his nose. "We're breaking up after the wedding, remember."

A sinking feeling settled in the pit of her stomach. "I know. But you want the family to think you're Mr. Responsible, right?"

"Right."

She pushed up from the bed, suddenly conscious of how naked she was without the nighttime darkness to conceal her. "We'll make it happen, I promise."

"Looking forward to it." He nodded, his eyes unreadable once more. "Hey...can I ask you something?"

"Sure." She looked around for her clothes but could only locate her underwear.

"Will you help me put a business plan together? You know, since Des is being such a hard-ass about it." He rolled his eyes as if the idea was a complete waste of time.

"Absolutely."

By the time Libby had showered and changed, Paul had gathered up her supplies from the previous night and was waiting by the door. They walked to the car in silence.

If it was only a night of fun between friends should she feel as though her heart wanted to drop through the floor? He kept his distance, helping her pack the box of now half-empty vodka bottles in her boot without so much as a brush of his hand against her. A far cry from the demanding, delicious touch he'd given her last night.

Libby bounced on her feet, words escaping her.

"I guess I'll see you soon," he said, standing back on the curb with his arms folded across his chest.

"Yeah, see you soon." She opened the car door and slid into the driver's seat.

Something told her each minute would be increasingly painful until she was in his arms again.

Chapter Ten

"Stop being such a baby!" Libby sat on a barstool at First, her laptop open in front of her and a half-finished cocktail next to it. She shook her head, sending copper curls bouncing around her face.

Paul gritted his teeth. "Do you really not see this is the stupidest thing ever? Now I know why so many businesses fail, it's not poor management...it's paperwork."

True to her word, Libby had set a time with him to work on the business plan for the mixology school idea. She'd come to the bar on a quiet Tuesday night, and they were brainstorming and working through her template as Paul tended to his duties serving the few customers who'd trickled in for a mid-week drink.

"Why should Des trust your idea will work without a plan?" She reached for her cocktail and sipped it, her eyes narrowed at him.

"Because I'm his brother...and it's a good idea."

"No, that's not how it works."

"Maybe because I'm not type A like you," he muttered under his breath as he polished a highball glass.

"Call me names if it makes you feel better, but we *will* finish this plan." She huffed. "Although you're making it harder than it needs to be."

"Because I don't like planning out every unimportant detail to the nth degree?" He reached for another glass. "I'm a creative person, Libby, not an accountant."

"That doesn't mean you can forgo the numbers side of things. Des is right to ask for this plan." She tapped at her computer. "You need to suck it up."

"You're exceptionally bossy, you know that, right?"

"Thank you." The genuine smile that lit up her face made him laugh; only Libby would consider that a compliment.

Truth was he felt out of his depth. Numbers and market analysis and contingency funds were so *not* his thing. The joy of his work came in creating something new, something exciting. He loved the idea of teaching people how to experiment, how to pair flavors, how to make drinks that got people talking.

But this activity had only showed him just how different he and Libby were. She had a business savvy unlike anything he'd ever seen before. She even put Des to shame. Her understanding and knowledge highlighted that he flew by the seat of his pants…with everything.

All of that should have made him want to run for the hills, but it didn't. And that terrified him.

"Okay." She tapped her nail against the bar for a moment, her lips pursed. "We need to talk about your pricing strategy."

"A hundred dollars."

"For the class? How did you come up with that?"

He opened the dishwasher and started stacking the dirty glasses into the top rack. "It seems like a nice round number."

"That you pulled out of your ass?" Libby shook her head. "You need to take this seriously, Paul."

"What I need is to run one of these nights and show Des how good I can be. You *know* I'm better with my hands. If he just gives me a chance—"

"He won't unless we get through this document." The exasperation in her tone made it clear she wasn't going to leave that stool unless he did what she said. "You asked for my help and I'm going to deliver it whether you like the process or not."

"You know, I can see a little of your father in you."

A deep pink flush rose up into her cheeks and she glared at him with the force of a thousand suns. "You did *not* just say that to me."

"Didn't I?" He raised a brow, enjoying knocking Libby off her high horse more than he should have.

Everything felt like a game with her, a challenge for him to seize. In the past, women had given in to him or he'd simply taken what he wanted. Even Sadie never challenged him outright—all her dissatisfaction came to fruition behind his back. Passive aggressive was her M.O.

But Libby stood her ground and dug her heels in, happy to argue until they were both blue in the face. It made his blood pump harder through his veins; she matched him. Butted heads with him. Pushed him and didn't take any of his shit.

"You know what makes me different than my dad?" she asked, folding her arms across her chest and giving him an eyeful of beautiful, creamy cleavage.

"What?" He slammed the dishwasher drawer shut and leaned on the bar.

"I don't push people because I think I know what's best for them. I push people I believe in, especially when I feel like they're slacking for no reason." She sighed. "I *do* believe in you Paul...and in your idea."

The words hit him as hard as a slap across the face. Now he understood why being with Libby felt different from all the other women he'd slept with. It wasn't just lust. It wasn't just attraction and tension and hormones. On some level he knew that she saw more in him than anyone else did. But that wasn't part of their arrangement.

"You're selling yourself short, and I'm not sure why." She peered at him, her copper-colored brows wrinkling above her tiny button nose. "You deserve more."

Wasn't that the exact reason Sadie had left him? Because she didn't think he had the potential to give her more, to give her what she craved. Success, affluence, status.

But Libby *believed* in him.

No, no, no. That's not how their deal was supposed to go down.

"I..." He opened his mouth, but his brain had no words; there wasn't a precedent for this situation. No one had said those things to him before.

Her eyes widened as she looked at him, waiting for a response that wasn't coming. "I uhhh...where is the ladies room?"

He pointed to the doors on the other side of the restaurant and she hopped off her stool, scurrying away like a mouse that had escaped a trap. Pink and red danced in the distance as her hair flapped against the back of her dress, her heels clicking loudly in the quiet restaurant.

"Dammit," he swore under his breath.

Why did she have to say those things to him? It was like taking a bite of the forbidden fruit, he could get addicted to her praise. To the way she looked at him as though he was the kind of man who wouldn't disappoint her.

That was fine in the bedroom, but not out here. Not in the real world where he knew he'd crush that hope right out of her if he was ever stupid enough to let her in.

He had to draw a line in the sand and fast.

Libby braced her hands against the bathroom countertop and stared at her reflection. On the outside she appeared calm; her cheeks had returned to their normal color and her gaze was steady. Inside, however, was another story entirely.

What the hell was she doing telling Paul how much she believed in him? They weren't in a real relationship. Hell, they weren't even really friends. Their arrangement was supposed to be a business deal and somehow sex had snuck in… now she was giving him some impassioned speech about how he deserved more in life.

"Stupid, stupid, stupid." She squeezed her eyes shut and forced herself to breathe slowly for ten counts.

All she had to do was go back out there and get down to business. That wouldn't be so hard, planning and strategizing were her strengths. And she wanted Paul's idea to succeed because it would help her business…it wasn't about him.

Yeah right, you're letting yourself be fooled. Multiple

orgasms should not make you forget why you don't go near guys like him.

Squaring her shoulders, she smoothed her hands down the front of her dress, adjusted the little bow at her waist, and touched up her pink lipstick.

Game face on.

But the second she walked back out into First's dining area her confidence melted like an ice cube on hot asphalt. A woman stood near her laptop, her forearms resting on the bar as an indecently short skirt rode up her long, lean legs. Miles of blond hair trailed down her back, gleaming like spun gold.

Paul grinned at the woman, his arms folded across his chest in a way that made his muscles bulge behind the tight confines of his black T-shirt. He laughed at something she said and raked a hand through his short, dark hair.

Bile rushed up in her throat as she approached. How many times had she watched this exact kind of scene play out with her ex while naively thinking that he loved her? Instead he'd been lapping up the attention, mentally picking out his next conquest while she believed they would be together forever.

"Libby," Paul said as she approached the bar. "This is Cassie. We backpacked around Europe together a few years ago."

"Far too long ago," Cassie said in a lilting Irish accent. "Although parts of that trip are still fuzzy. You drank me under the table back then."

"Still could now," he replied with a wink.

"Lovely to meet you." Libby stuck out her hand and Cassie shook it, smiling warmly. "Are you on holiday?"

"No I just moved here. Got sick of living in London

where it's gray and drizzly all the time. Paul kept telling me how wonderful Melbourne is so I thought I'd see for myself." She looked at Paul with such adoration that Libby felt like she might vomit.

"You'll like it here, Cass. Plenty of booze and partying." Paul grabbed a pint glass and held it under the Guinness tap. "How about a pint of the black stuff? It's on the house."

"You're a good man, Paul Chapman." Cassie readily accepted the glass of dark liquid and sipped. "But I'm done with the partying, to be honest. I think I'm ready to settle down for a while and just enjoy being here."

"You settling down, never!"

"You'd be surprised."

Libby didn't miss the look on Cassie's face, the yearning and wanting that she'd felt herself at one time. She'd come here for Paul, and he was completely oblivious. Fire ran through Libby's veins, jealousy burning like a wildfire out of control. She took a deep breath and tamped it down. Those kind of feelings had no place here.

"So, how do you two know each other?" Cassie asked.

An awkward pause filled the air.

"Libby is my girlfriend," Paul said eventually. "We've been going out for…"

"About a month," Libby filled in.

Cassie smiled—at least Libby assumed she was aiming for a smile, but it came out somewhere between that and a grimace. "I thought you didn't do relationships."

He rubbed the back of his neck and laughed. "I didn't. But people change, I guess."

An image flickered at the edge of Libby's mind as Paul swept his eyes over Cassie. The two of them in bed, drinking, partying. Young and wild and having the time of their lives. She steadied herself by putting a hand on the bar.

Paul's expression was guarded, his dark eyes revealing nothing. Did he still have feelings for Cassie? She would be here when their fake relationship dissolved, or would he try to break the rules and go back to her before then?

"I actually need to head off," Libby said, reaching for her laptop and folding it shut. "We can work on the plan another time."

"Sure." Paul nodded absently. "See you later."

As she walked out of the bar, heat prickled along her neck and scalp. She'd promised herself she'd never be in a position to feel like this again...and yet here she was. Wringing her hands and wondering what he'd do once she was gone. The sound of Paul and Cassie laughing haunted her as she fled.

It didn't matter, he could do whatever he liked. The boundaries had to be established, and she'd remember this moment when that time came.

Libby's hands shook as she put the finishing touch on the last of the custom cocktails. Thirty identical champagne flutes lined an ornate sideboard at Gracie's mother's house, each with the perfect amount of cherry puree and garnish.

She and Gracie had decided to debut Paul's creation at the pre-wedding kitchen tea. It would be a perfect opportunity to gauge feedback before the big day and make any final tweaks, if necessary. Libby had the feeling it would be a tough crowd: a mixture of Cecilia Greene's society friends and the very traditional Chapman family.

It would also be Libby's first time meeting Paul's extended family.

She could hardly believe it had been close to a month since they formed their arrangement. He'd slipped into her life quietly and seamlessly, but she already feared that his exit wouldn't be so unnoticeable, especially since they hadn't spoken after she'd left the bar abruptly a week ago.

"Are you okay? If you keep looking so nervous someone will mistake you for the bride." Gracie patted her on the shoulder.

"I'm fine. You look lovely, by the way."

Gracie wore a floaty red dress with huge, dangling earrings that chimed when she shook her head. Her dark curls were pinned up loosely, several tendrils falling down around her face.

"So do you. I'm so jealous of those heels."

Libby looked down to the towering emerald green stilettos on her feet. They had plaited straps and a delicate gold buckle at the ankle. "They're my good luck charms."

"You don't need them; everyone is going to love the cocktails." Gracie grinned, her eyes twinkling. "And if they don't, who cares? *I* love them and so does Des. By the way, he asked me to tell you to bring a few samples to the bar whenever you can. He wants to do a tasting session with a few of his regulars."

Progress. Libby clapped her hands together. "Great, I'll bring them around tonight."

"Paul must be so proud of you. I have a feeling your business is going to do very well." She winked.

The future for Libby Gal Cocktails was certainly looking brighter. After meeting with Des during the week, he'd agreed to take her on for a trial period. She'd drafted a press release, which had been picked up by a few Australian food bloggers and one online industry magazine. It wasn't world-wide domination, but it was a start.

Since then she'd been contacted by a few smaller restaurants who'd expressed interest in her product. They weren't as high profile as the ones she'd started out targeting, but they seemed passionate about trying new things, and she'd come to realize that was just as important as the size of a restaurant's reputation. Not to mention a thirst for creativity over celebrity endorsement.

"Thanks. I think he's proud," she said, forgetting for a moment that she had to play the role of happy girlfriend.

"Of course he is." Gracie shook her head, fiddling with the centerpiece in the middle of the table that would house all the food. "I can tell."

The bouquet of white and silver silk flowers had been sewn with a smattering of crystals that caught the afternoon light. A lace tablecloth covered the dark wood, and two large white letters—*G* and *D*—sat on either side of the centerpiece. In that moment, Libby understood why some people got caught up in the excitement of weddings.

Ordinary things seemed special because they carried the weight of a greater meaning. The letters weren't just *G* for golf and *D* for Delta. They represented the union of two people who loved each other enough to risk a lifetime of messy emotional entanglement.

Libby swallowed against the lump in her throat.

"You should see the way he looks at you," Gracie continued. "I've seen Paul around a *lot* of women. Believe me, he hasn't looked that way at any of them except you."

"What do you mean?" She didn't care, but a happy girlfriend would ask that question.

Yeah, keep telling yourself that.

"He gets this expression on his face when you're around. He looks...content." She gave Libby's shoulder a squeeze. "You make him happy. Even Des has noticed a change."

"Really?"

"He said the other night that Paul seems more invested in his work, he's more motivated. You've been a great influence on him." She drew Libby into a hug. "I'm so glad you two met."

A large stone settled in the pit of Libby's stomach. Gracie and Des—and Paul's parents—were such wonderful people, and she was lying to them over and over. They'd embraced her with such warmth and acceptance, she didn't know how she'd ever go back to the cold criticism of her own family once it was all over. These people didn't deserve to be lied to. The truth hovered on her tongue; she wanted to clear the air. Settle the score with her conscience.

But Paul had held up his end of the bargain, and now her product was going to be on the menu at First. She had to see it through to the end and hope that she'd be able to make it up to them.

"Don't look so worried." Gracie released her with a grin. "Everything will work out, trust me."

The doorbell rang, and within moments the Greene household was buzzing. Waiters had been hired to serve drinks from silver trays, including the special cocktails. No detail had been left unattended. Everything matched from the invitations to the name tags to the trimmings on the seats that lined the large dining area.

Games had been set up and a table had been cleared for presents, which was soon filled to bursting. Libby hung back, introducing herself to anyone who came near, but she didn't want to get too involved. After all, her relationship with Paul was due to expire in two weeks. It made her feel like a carton of milk.

An elegant woman with glossy blond hair dropped down into the chair next to Libby and slipped her feet out of a pair of low, sensible heels.

"I love your shoes," she said, looking forlornly at Libby's heels. "I miss high heels so much." She placed her hand over her stomach for a moment and sighed. Other than some dark shadows under her eyes, everything about her was perfectly polished. A diamond the size of a beach pebble sparkled on her left hand and matched the two smaller stones in her ears. "No one ever tells you how tired you get when you're pregnant."

"How far along are you?" Libby asked. The bump on the woman's stomach was small, and if she'd been wearing a flowy top you might not have been able to see it.

"Just over four months. Though it feels like even longer since I can't get through the night without needing to go to the toilet a hundred times. And don't get me started on the morning sickness." She cringed and tucked her hair behind an ear. "I don't get these women who say pregnancy makes them feel beautiful."

"You look lovely, if that means anything." Libby caught the attention of a passing waiter and grabbed a cocktail.

"Oh and I've been craving a drink like you would not believe." The woman shook her head. "But enough about my pregnancy woes. I'm Sadie."

Libby shook her hand. "Libby. How do you know Gracie?"

"I'm married to one of Desmond's cousins. I must admit I've only met Gracie on a few occasions, but it was very sweet of her to invite me."

"She's a lovely woman. Des has done well for himself."

Sadie nodded. "Indeed he has."

As if she'd heard her own name, Gracie wandered over. "Sadie, did Libby tell you she created these wonderful cocktails for us? We'll have to make you a special one, I made sure we had a bottle of non-alcoholic wine for you."

"You made them?" Sadie looked impressed. "They're so beautiful and I bet they taste divine. You girls really are making me jealous."

"I can't really take the credit." Libby said, shaking her head. "Paul was the one who put them together. I just made the special ingredient."

"Paul?" Sadie blinked.

"Oh, Des's brother. I assume you've met?" Libby sensed a change in the air around them as Sadie and Gracie exchanged looks.

"Libby is Paul's girlfriend," Gracie explained. "She's helping out with the drinks for the wedding."

"Oh." Sadie tried to smile but her lips made more of a grimace.

"I'm sorry to ditch you, Sadie, but I need to check on something in the kitchen. Libby, could you give me a hand?" Gracie shot her a look that said *now*.

"Of course. It was lovely to meet you, Sadie. I'm sure we'll bump into each other at the wedding."

Sadie nodded, but her eyes were focused on her lap.

"Is Paul's name a bad word or something?" Libby asked

as they threaded through the guests and stepped into the hallway.

"I'm surprised he hasn't told you." Gracie sighed. "It's quite awkward. Sadie and Paul used to date."

"That's odd, he's never mentioned it."

"Yeah, maybe he wasn't sure how to bring it up. Anyway, Sadie's a lovely girl but the whole thing makes family gatherings pretty uncomfortable. They'd been together for a few years, and everyone thought they were going to get serious. Then it turns out she'd been sleeping with his cousin."

So Sadie was the ex who cheated on him, but he'd never mentioned that it was with his *cousin*.

How awful knowing that she not only betrayed him, but that it was with a family member. Someone who should have put him first. Every time they had a family function he'd have to face the infidelity, the lies. It was a never-ending punishment.

No wonder he'd wanted someone by his side at the wedding.

"Oh my God, that's awful."

"Yeah, apparently he came home and found her packing her bags with his cousin standing right there." Gracie shook her head. "But I didn't want to exclude her, she *is* family, after all. I'm sorry, I would have mentioned it earlier but I assumed you knew."

"I didn't." Anguish turned over and over in her stomach. "It's an awful story. I feel terrible for him."

"Don't feel too bad." Gracie slung her arm around Libby's shoulders. "He's got you now."

"If you put your hand any higher I'm going to have to let my girlfriend know I cheated on her today," Paul said.

The older gentleman checking the inseam for Paul's tuxedo pants shook his head and muttered something to himself. The whole thing was a little too intimate for Paul's tastes. Not to mention that his junk had been touchy since his night with Libby. Any mention of her name caused a reel of X-rated memories to flood him, and that had…unsociable consequences.

But those thoughts quickly lead to thinking about Libby's declaration of belief in him at the bar…and he had no idea what to do with that.

"This is a professional operation, Mr. Chapman," the tailor said drily.

Des shot Paul a look. "Stay still and it'll be over in a moment."

"That's what she said." Noah grinned and ducked when Des's hand came flying toward him.

"Get all your jokes out now," Des warned. "Because I'll cause you a world of pain if you ruin my wedding."

"Lighten up, man." Noah slung an arm around Des's neck. "Gracie might have your balls in a sling once you sign the paperwork, but you're still ours for now."

"Paperwork has already been signed, Noah. It has to be done before the wedding."

"But you sign something on the day, isn't that why you have to have witnesses at the wedding?"

"It's basically a fake. If you haven't done the real paperwork before then the marriage isn't valid."

"What about Vegas weddings? Can't I get hammered

at the casino and then marry a stripper on a whim?" Noah shook his head. "What's the world coming to?"

"I think the laws are different in America," Des pointed out. "Your random stripper wife fantasy may come true yet."

"Just goes to show how much we know about weddings," Paul said, turning around and holding out his arms when the tailor instructed him to.

"I'll be happy when it's all over and we can go back to talking about things other than flower arrangements and speeches."

Paul finished up with the tailor and then swapped places with Des. He itched to change out of the suit and back into his jeans, but they had at least another twenty minutes of checking and measuring to ensure the custom tuxedos were perfect for the big day.

"How do you think Libby will handle seeing Sadie at the wedding?" Noah asked.

Paul blinked. "What do you mean?"

"Well, it's always unbearably awkward when she and Mich—"

Paul held up a hand.

"He who shall not be named," Noah said, making quotation marks with his fingers, "end up in the same room as you."

"She doesn't need to meet Sadie." Paul folded his arms across his chest. "I've done pretty well avoiding her all this time; there's no reason that can't continue."

Noah frowned. "You have to deal with it at some point."

"You're one to judge; when was the last time you spoke with your mother's family?"

Noah's face hardened, and Paul immediately regretted

the words. His situation was nothing compared to what Noah went through growing up. Calling that out was just a dick move.

"I didn't mean that," Paul said, sighing. "Things are so new with Libby, I don't want to screw things up by delving into my fucked-up history with Sadie and that letch who happens to be related to us."

The truth in his words unsettled Paul. He hadn't told Libby the whole situation with Sadie because he didn't want her pity. Asking her to pretend to date him was a tactical move, one he'd put aside his pride for. He didn't need to rub salt into the wound by telling her that his ex had left him for an upgraded version.

"So you haven't told her about Sadie," Noah pressed. "Are you crazy? You're just going to let her find out on her own?"

Paul shrugged. "I don't know what the big deal is, I don't have to tell her everything."

"When she finds out she'll know that you're keeping things from her. You'll be in the doghouse, my friend." Noah nodded sagely.

"And you know this from your string of successful relationships with women?" Paul quipped.

"Sticks and stones. I grew up with three foster sisters. I *know* women."

Des looked over his shoulder, earning himself a stern word from the tailor to keep still. "They're having a baby— she's not going anywhere and neither is he. You have to get over it. It blows, but that's reality. Tell her Sadie will be there."

"Unless you're just keeping Libby around for a bit of fun…" Noah looked at Paul with a glint in his eye. He knew exactly how to push his buttons. "I mean, that's more your style, isn't it?"

"She's *not* just a bit of fun," he said the words so vehemently that his whole body tensed like he was bracing himself for a physical blow.

The thought had been weighing on him all week. The fact that they would be parting ways in two short weeks had settled over him like a dark cloud and dampened any pleasure he should be feeling about proving Sadie and his family wrong.

This is not how you're supposed to feel about a fake girlfriend. You're not supposed to feel anything.

Maybe it was a mistake sleeping with her. He'd expected that it would go the same as with any of the other women he'd bedded in the last few years wherein he'd feel less interested afterward, not more.

He certainly never stewed over the idea that the relationship would end. But thinking past the wedding to when he and Libby would be no more was like looking into a bottomless pit. It wasn't a place he wanted to go and yet confronting the way he felt about her was equally unappealing. Why couldn't she just be like everyone else?

"You're hooked, man." Noah clapped a hand on his back. "She's working her lady voodoo on you *bad*!"

"I haven't seen him like this in a long time." Des grinned. "I got that look on my face when I met Gracie. Be warned, bro, it's a slippery slope."

It was indeed a slippery slope, and he was sliding headfirst at full speed.

Chapter Eleven

Thanks to Gracie's mother's militant event planning, the kitchen tea was packed with activities, meaning Libby didn't have time to think about her recent discovery. She threw herself into helping coordinate the games and assisting Cecilia, Gracie, and Gracie's sister, Emmaline, wherever possible.

"Thank you for your help today, dear," Cecilia said, motioning for one of the caterers to come so she could hand them an envelope.

"The extra pair of hands was great." Emmaline smiled as she stuffed the crumpled wrapping paper into a garbage bag. "Mother wanted to get people in to run the whole thing, but I thought it would feel more personal if we did it as a family."

"That's sweet," Libby replied, collecting a handful of paper and handing it over.

A few guests remained, including Sadie who looked

as though she wanted to curl up on the couch and go to sleep. While the other women occupied themselves, Libby watched Sadie talking to a few of Paul's aunts. She couldn't imagine Sadie and Paul together the way she had when she'd seen him with Cassie the other night.

Sadie seemed nice, but she looked so formal, so polished. Nothing like the kind of girl Paul would date.

But what did she know? The reason she was dating Paul was to help her business, and he'd suggested it because there was something in it for him…not because he was attracted to her.

Why do you care if he's attracted to you? It's not a requirement for the job.

But it had become clear that his opinion did matter and that Libby had crossed the line by daring to feel sorry for him upon discovering the truth about his ex…not to mention her recent idiotic display of truth. They'd said up front that emotions were to be kept completely out of it. She couldn't breathe a word of this to Paul.

Libby picked up a couple of empty teacups and carried them into the kitchen to be washed. The catering crew had done most of the cleaning, and the dishwasher whirred as it churned through yet another batch of dishes. She placed the cups on the counter.

As she went to leave the kitchen she heard her name, though it was obvious the person was talking about her and not to her. Flattening her back against the wall next to the alcove that lead to the hallway, she strained to listen above the gush of water in the dishwasher.

"The redhead," the first voice said. "That's his new girlfriend."

"No way. He finally stopped fucking his way from here to kingdom come?"

"Maybe she'll be able to do what I couldn't." The first voice definitely belonged to Sadie.

"What, tame him? Please. Some people aren't meant to be the settle-down, get-married type. Hell, he wasn't even the hold-a-job type…if it wasn't for his brother, he'd still be out of work and mooching off Zia Leone."

"I tried so hard to encourage him to do something with his life." Sadie's voice wavered.

"Don't cry."

"It's these bloody hormones."

"That's the reason you're upset now, not because of Paul. You made the right choice to be with Michael instead."

"You have to say that, he's your brother."

"I believe it."

"I shouldn't have cheated on Paul."

"Sure, but he more than made up for it after you left by screwing anything that could walk."

Libby's hands trembled in front of her. How *dare* they talk about him like that. Judging by how he'd treated her in the last month *and* considering they weren't even in a real relationship, Libby had zero doubt in her mind that he'd been a great boyfriend to Sadie. Perhaps he hadn't lived up to everyone's expectations, but who would even try with people like that putting you down? These people were his family and yet they talked about him as though he were the scum of the earth.

And she knew *exactly* what it was like to have your own family push you into the ground. No one should have to experience that.

"You chose right, Sadie," the second voice said. "Paul's a lost cause, but good luck to this girl in trying to change him."

Sucking in a breath, Libby pulled back her shoulders and walked into the hallway.

"For the record, I like Paul just the way he is," she said, not even pausing to let them close their mouths. "He's a wonderful, supportive boyfriend and I wouldn't be with him if all I wanted was to turn him into someone else."

Sadie's face paled and the girl next to her, who Libby assumed was another of Paul's cousins, blinked rapidly. Neither girl said anything to fill the void.

"And, for the record," she said, putting her hands on her hips. Adrenaline coursed through her, the high from standing up for Paul fueling her words. "We're thinking about getting married because he's never been so happy, and neither have I."

She regretted the words as soon as they came out of her mouth, even more so when she realized that Paul's mother had walked into earshot. Libby wished the floor would open up and swallow her whole, so she could stew over her bad life decisions in solitude.

"Married?" The look on Leone's face was like a stake through Libby's heart. Paul was going to *kill* her.

"We're just talking about it," she said, trying to smooth the situation over. "It was supposed to be private, but it just…popped out."

Sadie blanched. "He told me marriage was old-fashioned."

Libby shrugged, grappling for how to recover. She had to get to Paul and tell him what she'd done so they could come up with a solution. But how could she tell him that without revealing what his family was saying about him be-hind his back?

Her stomach swished, the floor tilting beneath her feet. What had she done?

Leone looked so excited Libby wondered if she might spontaneously combust. She rushed over and enveloped Libby into a tight hug. "This is wonderful news!"

"You have to keep it a secret," Libby begged. "He'll be mad if he finds out I mentioned it without consulting him first."

Or even alerting him to this mystical fact.

"You have my word," Leone said. "I won't make a peep."

Now all Libby had to do was figure out how to tell Paul that she'd made things worse for him.

P aul turned his mobile over in his hands, contemplating what to do about Libby. Guilt weighed on him. Maybe Noah and Des were right. He *should* have told her the full story about Sadie.

But the last thing he wanted was her pitying him or, God forbid, saying something at the wedding. He didn't need any-one feeling sorry for him. The whole point of his "relation-ship" with Libby was to change that power dynamic. Except now these complicated feelings of guilt and obligation had clawed their way in—along with a few other, more primal feelings—and he was debating how to break the news to her.

He held his thumb over her number when a knock sounded at his door. Libby stood on his doorstep as if ma-terialized from his thoughts. Her long, copper-colored hair floated around bare shoulders, draping over the top of a strapless dress in shades of pale blue and yellow.

"Don't you look like a fantasy?" He looked her up and down, taking in the details he'd come to expect from her. The shoes matched perfectly with the tiny green leaves on the flower pattern of her dress.

It was that level of attention and care which made her such a fantastic businesswoman. Everything she did was thought out to the very last detail...even if it did drive him crazy when she expected the same from him.

"Hey, I hope it's okay that I dropped by without calling first." She stepped through the door, her hands knotted in front of her.

"Of course."

"So we had the kitchen tea today," she said, walking through to the living room and dropping down onto the couch. She slipped her feet out of her heels and rubbed at a mark on her ankle where the strap had bitten into her skin.

"What's the point of that again?" Paul took the seat across from her.

"It's like a wedding shower. Traditionally people buy gifts for the kitchen, but these days it's just all the women getting together to chat about the wedding and play games." She tapped her fingertip to her chin. "Think of it as a super tame version of a hen's party."

"No male strippers then?"

She laughed and shook her head. "No strippers, no penis-shaped straws or lollipops."

He stared at her. "Girls really have that?"

"Oh yeah, I've even seen cupcakes decorated with them at one hen's party."

"I feel cheated."

"I don't prefer the cupcake if that's what you're worried about." A cheeky smile pulled up on her lips.

"Damn straight."

Silence settled over them and again Libby knotted her hands. Underneath the jokes and her beautiful smile he sensed a wariness in her.

"I met some interesting people at the kitchen tea." She sucked on her lower lip, her eyes avoiding his.

Paul's stomach dropped. It would be just his luck if she met Sadie today after he'd come close to calling her and fessing up.

"Anyone in particular?"

"I met your ex, Paul." She looked up and nodded slowly. "I was chatting with her, but I had no idea who she was. Then Gracie introduced me as your girlfriend and she filled me in afterward. I never realized the guy she cheated with was your cousin."

He watched her face, waiting for the pity. Waiting for any sign that she thought him pathetic for being duped by Sadie and his cousin.

"You can understand why I wasn't keen to share those details," he said drily, interlacing his fingers behind his head.

She nodded. "I do understand but…"

"But?" he asked, his defenses rising like great shadows around him.

He fought the urge to push up from his chair and stalk out of the house. Storming off was his usual way of dealing with problems. Lord knew how many times he'd walked away from his brother or his parents in such a manner. If he was being honest with himself, he'd done it a number of times to Sadie as well.

Libby deserved more than that. He'd dragged her into his problems by keeping information from her. She shouldn't have to deal with his temper as well.

"It would have been better if I'd known. I was taken by surprise." She was working up to something—her leg bounced and she fiddled with the hem of her dress, picking at some invisible flaw.

He nodded, gritting his teeth. "I didn't want to put you in that position."

"I know." She sucked in a breath, her chest rising and falling. She continued to pick at her dress.

"What's wrong, Libby? Did she say something to you?"

"It wasn't what *she* said." Libby looked up, her brows creased as she chewed on her lip.

"I don't understand."

"I said something, Paul. Something bad." The anguish on her face was killing him.

"Spit it out. I can't help if you don't tell me what's going on." The hypocrisy of his statement wasn't lost on him, but right now all he wanted was to wipe the tension from her face.

"I overheard Sadie talking with someone, I didn't catch her name. Some things were said, things that weren't true and I just…reacted."

The muscles in his neck bunched, his hands curled into fists. He knew *exactly* who Libby was talking about—Miss Goody-Two-Shoes Gina who always looked down her nose at him. She and Sadie stuck to each other like Tweedledum and Tweedledee. Gina thought her brother was God's gift and that no one else in the family deserved what he did.

They took, took, took without regard to anyone else.

"What did they say?" He ground the question out through clenched teeth.

"It doesn't matter...all you need to know is that I wanted to stick up for you."

"*What* did they say?" Humiliation coursed through him, curling in his gut like a poisonous snake.

Libby ran a hand through her hair. "I don't want to repeat it."

He sat still as a statue, shutting down his emotions. Packing them all into a tight ball and pushing them deep down as he'd done day after day since Sadie left. He knew eventually the pain would stop, but every so often something happened to split him apart, and it would all come tumbling out if he wasn't careful.

He looked at the scar on his right hand, the one he'd gotten when he put his fist through a wall after bumping into Sadie and his cousin right before they got married.

"Tell me, Libby." He drew a slow breath. "I need to know."

"You're just going to torture yourself with it." She shook her head. "I told them that you're perfect just the way you are. That we're happy together and I don't want to change a single thing about you."

He felt a "but" coming on.

"But," she said, steadying her breathing. "Something else kind of slipped out."

"What?"

"I told them..." She grimaced.

"God, Libby, you're killing me. Spit it out."

"I told them we were thinking about getting married."

The words seemed to suck the life out of the room, turning it into a vacuum. His head pounded, the ramifications of her words flying at him thick and fast like a swarm of wasps.

He shook his head. "Say that again?"

Her face begged him not to make her repeat the admission, but he held his tongue until she sighed, defeated. "I told them we were thinking about getting married."

He gaped at her. "What on earth possessed you to do that?"

"I couldn't listen to them say these things that were untrue and…" She swallowed. "Unkind. You deserve better than that, and I got so angry that I confronted them. It slipped out."

"How does the invention of a marriage proposal simply slip out?"

For someone who claimed to have no interest in long-term relationships it didn't exactly seem like a go-to defensive move. Unless of course his wretched cousin and cheating ex were saying he wasn't marriage material. It wasn't exactly a stretch.

His hands curled around the arms of the sofa, fingertips rubbing against the beginnings of a split in the worn leather.

"I don't know," she said, her eyes wide and blank.

He leaned forward, bracing his forearms on his knees. The old Paul would have suspected Libby of using this situation to manipulate an outcome, force him down a specific path. But he knew her. *Really* knew her.

She wasn't that kind of girl, and she'd said she believed in him. Maybe she was just trying to protect him?

Libby hung her head. "I'm mortified."

He wanted to say something to comfort her, assure her

that it would be okay, but the combative emotions swirling within him prevented any words from coming out. He wanted to give her the benefit of the doubt, but the lie had posed a whole new set of complications. Especially if word got back to his parents that the dreaded *M* word had been uttered.

The clock on his wall ticked loudly, counting the stretch of silent shock.

Much to his confusion, he wasn't totally repelled by the idea that people thought he and Libby would be married. Since she'd said those damning words he'd been waiting for the dread to come…but it hadn't. Confusion, yes. Remorse for digging himself into a giant hole, probably. But dread? No.

Her fists clenched and unclenched in her lap. "I'm so sorry, Paul. I really don't know what came over me."

At this point he was more annoyed with his own lack of reaction than he was with her. This was exactly the kind of thing that should make him want to run for the hills but instead he sat there, wishing he could ease her pain. Feeling bad for her that she'd been put in a situation where she needed to use such a preposterous lie to defend him.

It was official. Paul Chapman was broken.

What happened to drawing a line in the sand?

"Say something," she said, her hazel eyes burning into him. Her tongue darted out to moisten her lips as she hovered at the edge of the sofa, her dress spread out like frosting on a cupcake.

"You were defending my honor," he said, a laugh bubbling up from nowhere. Broken *and* crazy, what a combination.

She looked at him like he'd sprouted antennae and had started talking an alien language. "It's not funny."

"No, it's ridiculous."

He should be mad. Looking at all the facts, she'd made his life a whole lot harder. How were they going to explain the engagement away without making either one of them look bad?

But the idea of Libby getting so worked up trying to defend him that she'd blurted out this completely insane lie…well, it warmed something inside him. Some cold part that had been frozen and packed away long ago.

"We'll make it work." He stood and held out a hand to Libby to help her up from her chair. "We don't have much choice now."

"You're not mad?" She grabbed his hand and followed him into the kitchen.

He shrugged. "Being mad is not going to fix the situation."

Not only was he *not* mad, but the gesture touched him in some strange, illogical way. That little nugget of information, however, would follow him to the grave.

"I'm not that person who does insane things on a whim."

"You dropped out of med school to start your own business despite having no support from your family. That sounds pretty insane to me." He turned on his coffee machine and grabbed two cups from the cupboard.

"Insane, maybe. On a whim…no. I'd been plotting a way to get out of med school since the first day of the course." A ghost of a smile crossed her face.

"So you favor planned insanity over the spontaneous kind?" he quipped. "Let me make sure I understand what happened. You told Sadie and Gina we're getting married, right? Was anyone else there?"

"Your mother." She looked down at her lap.

Paul cringed. "Okay, so it's safe to assume the whole family knows."

"I made her promise not to tell anyone."

The sincerity radiating from her face was touching. But she clearly knew nothing about the way the Chapman family operated.

"That promise is about as solid as cotton candy." He held a cup under the spout on the coffee machine, and the scent of freshly ground beans filled the air. "I guarantee you, by now everyone believes we're getting married."

"I told them we were *thinking* about it." She accepted a cup from him and blew on the steam.

"How did my mother react?"

She grimaced, pressing a palm to her forehead. "Like I'd announced that unicorns had been sent to make all her problems go away."

He gave her a pointed look.

"Okay fine, so they think we're getting married. What do we do?" She sipped her cup, a line forming between her brows. "We're supposed to break up after the wedding. Won't it be worse if we're supposedly engaged?"

Paul swallowed against the distaste in his mouth. He knew their time was coming to an end, but he couldn't seem to think about it without his body repelling the idea.

Of all the things you should be worried about with this situation…it's not that.

"It will, but that's what we have to work with now." He finished making his coffee and carried it to the kitchen bench.

She nodded, her fingertip tracing the rim of her cup. Silence settled over them; there wasn't much more to say on the issue of their sudden "engagement." Libby had done the right thing by coming to him straightaway instead of letting him find out by the inevitable phone call that would come in the morning.

"Anyway, I've got bigger things to focus on," he said.

"Like what?" Libby's face was a mask of relief at the change of topic.

"I've been working on the business plan. You're right, I do need to take it seriously…even if I think all the detail is stupid."

She grinned. "I'm glad you came to that conclusion all by yourself."

"I'm sick of not going for things that I want." He nodded, as if convincing himself. "I want this, I *know* it's a good idea, and it will bring in more money for First. I'm the best person to do it since I'm way more charming than Des and Noah."

Feelings warred within him: pride, fear, hope, and excitement. All battling for control. He had to channel them into something before he blurted out that he had feelings for her. That their "relationship" had changed him already…for the better.

"You're smarter than you give yourself credit for," she said, her face sincere for a moment before she realized what she'd said. "But you're not smarter than me."

"Maybe not when it comes to business." He took the cup from her hands and set it down on the bench. "But I'm smarter when it comes to other things."

"Like what?" she whispered.

"Sex."

"That's all you want me for, isn't it?" She laughed as if the statement was a joke, but he caught the uncertain flicker in her eyes.

He never wanted her to feel like that. Sure, he couldn't give her anything more…but it wasn't all she was worth. Not by a long shot.

He brushed her hair over one bare shoulder, trailing his fingers along her skin. His blood buzzed at the sharp intake of her breath, sending all the pressure rushing south. Goosebumps rippled across her skin where his fingers had been, like proof of his touch.

"You inspire me, Libby," he said, sliding his hand up her neck to cup the back of her head.

"I do?" She tilted her face up to his, her hazel eyes bright and wide.

"You're so ambitious and driven." He pressed his lips to her jaw. "You don't take any shit, but you've got a good heart."

"I think that's the nicest thing anyone has ever said about me." She laughed, narrowing her eyes at him in mock scrutiny. "You're trying to get me into bed again, aren't you?"

"We don't have to make it to the bed." He hoisted her up and carried her to the dining table.

"You know that girl Cassie came here for you." The words slipped out as he set her down.

"What?" He shook his head.

"She moved to Australia for you."

Paul raked a hand through his hair and rubbed the nape of his neck. "No, she didn't. She's been sick of London for a while, and I said she should come here because the weather is nice."

"How long after you said that did she move?"

"I don't know." He shrugged. "A month."

"Had you ever said it before?"

"Well…" He frowned, his eyes dropping to the ground as he tried to recall. "No."

"So she came here as soon as you said she should."

"You're making something out of nothing. We didn't have a relationship or anything, we were just backpacking and barhopping. It wasn't serious."

"I think she wanted it to be."

"How do you know that?"

Cassie had known from the start that he was on the rebound from Sadie when they'd met. He'd taken the money he'd saved up for her ring and spent it on three months of travel and denial. Cassie was a temporary thing, a way to drown his sorrows, and he'd been nothing but honest about that.

"I saw the way she looked at you, Paul. She came here for you, and you're absolutely clueless." Libby swung her legs back and forth. "Did you promise her the world?"

"To get her into bed? No, she knew *exactly* what she was getting into." How could Libby think he'd lie just to sleep with someone? "It's not my fault if she wants more."

"Well, whether or not you were up-front with her, she has feelings for you." Libby swallowed and shrugged, her face neutral. "Maybe you should go and talk to her after we 'break up.'"

"I'm not interested in Cassie…not like that. Not any-more. She's just a friend." He paused for a moment, watching the way her eyes flicked over his face as if she was looking for something. "You're jealous."

"I am not!" She went to jump down from the table but he pinned her there with a hand on either side of her thighs.

"You're totally *jealous*." He laughed and Libby's face flamed as red as her hair.

"You're not God's gift to women, you know," she grumbled. "But honestly, your ego is fascinating. I've never seen anything so big before."

"You know, that's not the first time someone has said that to me." He grinned and she swatted at him, narrowly missing his cheek.

"I stuck up for you, and this is the thanks I get?"

"Yep." His hands ran along her thighs, pushing up the fabric of her dress. "You wouldn't like it if I made it easy for you."

"Bullshit. I would very much enjoy life if you made it easier for me."

"You have many great skills, Tiger. But lying isn't one of them."

She locked her hands down over his, preventing him from going higher. "Many great skills, you say. Care to elaborate?"

"You've got a talented mouth."

She rolled her eyes.

"You know, since you speak so eloquently," he said. "And beautiful hands."

"Don't feed me all that crap you've used on other girls." She brushed his hands away. "I'm different, and I won't fall for it."

Didn't he know it? Libby was so far from his realm of experience that he may as well be starting from scratch.

But that's what she did to him. She'd broken down all his long-held beliefs—that he was happy taking the easy road through life, that he didn't want to be with anyone for more than a night—and systematically made him question the existence he'd created for himself.

"I know you're different." He shoved his hands into his pockets. "That's why you're still here."

She bit down on her lip and looked away. "You better not get attached to me."

"Wouldn't dream of it."

"I'm not going to change my mind on the relationship thing," she said, but her voice wavered ever so slightly. "I'm not interested in being tied to someone until we both hate each other. It's better to enjoy the good bits while they last and move on before it hurts too much. That's why I pointed out the thing about Cassie…you know, so you can talk to her after we break up."

"Right." He nodded, unsure what to do with the barrier she was desperately trying to put between them.

At one point he'd have been thrilled for a woman to keep things casual, but being with Libby had started to change him. He wanted more out of life than to cruise through without being committed to anyone or anything. He *deserved* more…she'd made him see that.

He didn't have to be the man his family thought he was. He would change, not to prove they were wrong but to prove *he'd* been wrong.

"I like you a lot, Paul." She touched his face, the gentle pressure of her fingertips zinging through him like bolts of electricity. "But I can't feel anything more than that. I won't let myself."

"You don't need to reassure me." He brought his hands back to her legs and parted them so he could stand closer to her.

The pressure of her thighs against his hips sent delicious heat through him. He ached for her, body and soul. But he'd only allow himself to fulfill one of those needs. He wouldn't ever tell her how he felt knowing she would walk away.

He wasn't going to have his heart broken again.

Chapter Twelve

The closer Gracie and Des's wedding drew, the heavier the pit in Libby's stomach. What was supposed to be a simple solution to a business problem had turned into a complicated personal conundrum. So much for leaving sex and emotion out of it. She'd failed spectacularly at the first one and was slipping down a steep ravine into the second.

The suitcase on her bed gaped at her like a big hungry mouth. She'd started packing half an hour ago, yet not a single item of clothing had made it into her luggage. The wedding was tomorrow; she had to pull herself together.

Pick a dress, match the shoes, find a pair of earrings. It's not that hard.

Libby glared at the two dresses that hung on the doors of her antique armoire. Decision paralysis was so *not* her thing, yet she couldn't seem to make a choice. Picking the dress meant packing her things, which meant getting in her car and driving all the way to the Yarra Valley…and seeing

Paul.

Her stomach churned. Since her big confession she'd been in a spin, and her mind refused to concentrate. Her ambition had deserted her, and she had the mental acuity of a stuffed llama. Even her motor skills were off. She'd shattered a wineglass on the kitchen faucet and dropped a fresh vase of flowers all over the carpet in her office.

Not exactly the picture of a put-together businesswoman.

"Come on," she muttered to herself as she studied the dresses. "Just do it."

The first one was sexy, backless, and black; it wasn't her usual style but she knew Paul would love it. The second was a bold pink and yellow 50s-style full-skirted number, definitely in her comfort zone.

She took a deep breath and snatched the black dress from her armoire, folding it in tissue and packing it before she could change her mind. She matched a pair of nude heels and a set of vintage enamel jewelry quickly, doing her hardest not to think about Paul.

Talk about a lesson in futility. Trying not to think about Paul was like trying not to blink…or breathe.

No matter how many times she mentioned the looming deadline of their relationship—*and* noticed how Paul seized up—she couldn't force reality to sink in. Would it be so bad to let things linger on and see if what they had extended beyond the wedding?

The slam of a car door outside caught her attention, and a moment later the doorbell rang. As soon as Libby stepped into the hallway she could see the shiny red paint on her father's convertible through the front window. Perfect. A heaping of fatherly guilt was exactly what she needed right now—not.

She opened the door but blocked the entrance. "Dad."

"Is that thug boyfriend of yours here to kick me out this time?" her father drawled.

Libby pursed her lips and stood rooted to the ground. "No."

"Do I need to ask for an invitation inside my own property?"

Ah, that old chestnut. The quicker Libby Gal Cocktails took off the sooner she could take that important step toward independence, getting out from under her father's thumb. She held the door open and waited for him to enter without saying the words, since it was clear he wasn't going to leave quietly.

"What do you want? I'm going away for the weekend, and I need to leave soon." She stood in the entrance and pressed her fingers to her temples.

"You used to speak to me as though I were the most important person in the world," her father said, looking—for possibly the first time ever—regretful. "What changed?"

"Maybe it's because I realized I wasn't the most important person in *your* world." She swallowed, blinking as tears pricked the backs of her eyes. She wouldn't give him the satisfaction of seeing her cry. "And that I never would be."

"That hurts, Libby." He shook his head. "Don't you see I want what's best for you?"

"How do you know what's best for me? I wonder at times if you know anything about me."

The muscle in his neck corded. "How can you say that?"

"What's my favorite food?" Her voice cracked and she cursed herself internally. "Or my favorite color?"

"Pink?" He shrugged. "What does it matter?"

"My favorite color is green, Dad. It always has been." She let out a sigh. "It matters because sometimes I think you wish I'd never been born."

The words sucked the life out of the room. Admitting her longest-held, most shameful fear aloud made the world feel colorless.

Her father blinked, genuine shock registering on his face. He brushed a hand through his hair, the mostly gray strands slipping through his fingers and springing back into place. He'd been a redhead, too, many moons ago. As a young girl she'd loved that they shared such a distinctive feature, like it was proof that she was his daughter. Proof her young heart had desperately needed when he acted as though she meant nothing.

"You know that your mother and I weren't planning to have children, but that doesn't mean I regret it."

"Don't you? I can't remember a time when you and Mum didn't fight or say horrible things to each other when you thought I couldn't hear."

His thick brows wrinkled. "Your mother and I should never have gotten married. We did it to provide for you, but I fear it only made your childhood harder."

"But then you both left, and you got remarried." The words tumbled like an avalanche. "You moved on...from me."

"I never moved on from you, and neither did your mother."

Libby's head pounded, the pain from her lonely childhood coursing through her body as fresh as it was when she found out her mother was having another child. A child who would have the happy life and the happy parents she'd been denied.

"Yes, you did. You moved away and I had to live with mum and her new husband. Then she sent me to you when she got pregnant, like I was being replaced. Instead of being my dad you sent me away as well!"

"Boarding school was a good option for you. I knew it would set you up for success. It wasn't because I didn't want you around." He shook his head as though she was talking gibberish. "You had so much potential, I wanted you to harness it. I wanted you to do great things."

"And to reach my potential I *have* to go back to med school?"

Silence. "What's the point of making flavored alcohol?"

Libby blinked. No one had ever asked her that before. The cold creep of doubt coiled in the pit of her stomach, winding its way up and over her heart.

"My product is fun, it's girlie. It celebrates women."

"By getting them drunk on cheap toxic cordials?"

She reeled as if he'd slapped her across the face.

"If you finished med school you could save people's lives, Libby. Isn't that a more worthy dream to have?"

She knew that her business was so much more than her father would ever see. She'd already drawn up plans to use her business plan to help other women realize their dream of working for themselves, of being financially independent. Her chest squeezed.

How could she ever show other women how to be independent when she lived in her father's house and had a fake boyfriend? In her desperation to succeed she'd lost sight of why she wanted to run her own business in the first place.

"I understand I'm living in your house, and I'm grateful for having a roof over my head. But that doesn't mean you get to control me or choose my fate." She squared her shoulders and sucked in a deep breath. "Your dream is not *my* dream. I hope one day you can accept that."

It shouldn't get to her—she'd seen him belittle her mother a thousand times before—but it hurt as much as if he'd kicked her to the ground. She had no hope of pleasing him, not now. Not ever.

Which was precisely the reason she'd never put herself in that position again. It was easy to avoid being hurt if she did her own thing, if she lived life for herself. Alone.

People couldn't hurt you if you kept them at a distance.

Paul carried box after box out to the car; who knew there could be so much "stuff" to take to a wedding. Everything had been delivered to his parents' house, and he was doing his brotherly duty to help get it all to the vineyard where the wedding would be held. Bonbonnière, place cards, table decorations, and God only knew what else.

He was sure, despite his limited experience, that the key to a happy marriage wasn't finding the perfect font for the seating lists.

"You look very deep in thought." His mother appeared beside him holding a small clear box with the wedding cake topper. She leaned in to his boot and tucked it into a carton containing other random bits and pieces.

"I was wondering if all weddings require three cars full of material items. I would have thought the bride and groom would be enough." He packed the last box in and checked to make sure everything was secure. The last thing he needed was to break two hundred tiny bottles of vodka.

"It's easy to get caught up in the details," she said, smiling wistfully. "Our wedding cake had over a hundred individual flowers made out of icing. It looked so beautiful."

"Yes, but did it taste good?"

"Who knows? I was so nervous I didn't eat a thing all night. I almost fainted after we got back to the hotel because I was so hungry."

"What a waste."

She patted his arm and shook her head. "It wasn't a waste. I wouldn't change a thing if I had to do it over again."

She hovered, her hands fidgeting with the fine gold chain at her neck. The cross dangling from it glinted in the afternoon light, winking at him as if it had a secret. That could only mean one thing. She had something important to say.

"Spit it out, Ma."

"I'm really glad you and Libby are getting engaged." Her eyes glimmered, her fingers fluttering at her neck. "It makes me so happy to see my boys finding love."

Shit. He'd been avoiding this conversation with her ever since Libby had confessed her little white lie…well, her small lie amongst a much bigger one.

"She wasn't supposed to say anything—it's not official yet." He thrust his fingers through his hair and tried to come up with a way to get out of talking to his mother about it. "Anyway, this is Des and Gracie's weekend. I don't want to steal their thunder."

"You're not. Des is so happy for you."

He sighed. "You told him? I thought Libby said you'd

promised to keep it a secret."

Her lips pulled up into a sheepish smile. "It's just one person."

"So you didn't tell Dad then? Or Zia Marcella?" He raised a brow. "Or Mrs. Lawson from down the street?"

"I didn't tell Mrs. Lawson," she admitted. "But yes, I told your father and Zia Marcella. I can't help it, I'm so excited."

"You promised Libby and then you went against your word."

"Oh, do you think she'll be mad?" His mother looked genuinely stricken. "I thought it wouldn't matter if you were planning it already."

It wouldn't, if they were in a real relationship or had any intention of ever getting married. But they'd be splitting up in a few days' time...just as soon as the wedding was over and his business idea had come to fruition.

"She won't be mad." He couldn't make his mother feel guilty when he was the one lying and fooling everyone.

"Good. Because I have a gift for her." She reached into her pocket and pulled out a small velvet box.

A cold trickle of fear ran down his spine. "What is that?"

She opened the box and amongst the cushy interior sat a band of diamonds. Each stone was shaped like a double-ended teardrop, the gaps dotted with tiny red rubies, making the ring look more like a wreath than a typical wedding ring.

"This belonged to my great grandmother," she said, tracing a finger over it. "I've been saving it for when you found the right girl."

"You never showed me this when I was with Sadie." The words stuck in his throat.

"You never said you were going to marry her."

"Technically I haven't asked Libby yet, either." At least there was one thing he could say without lying. "And why didn't you give it to Des?"

"I know it probably seems like I'm hard on you all the time, but I was like you when I was younger." His mother wrapped her arm around his waist and rested her head on his shoulder. "I didn't know what I wanted to do with my life and your *nonno* was always frustrated with me because I wanted to explore and see the world. He just wanted me to settle down."

"I can't imagine it."

She laughed. "I'm hard on you because I know you have greatness in you, Paul. But, like me, you need a good shove sometimes."

"You're too little to push me around." He teased her to make light of the emotion battling inside him. His mother had never given him any indication that she understood him on such a deep level, let alone that she had been the same way herself.

"Sometimes it takes the right person to help us see our potential. I think Libby is that person for you...that's why I want you to give her the family ring."

His chest seized, guilt crushing down on him like a boulder. It was official; he'd easily take the title of worst son in the world. Jesus, why had he been so stupid to lie to his whole family?

"Ask her, Paolo. Make it official. Girls like that don't come along every day."

Didn't he know it? But wondering about what could be was pointless when he'd been down this road before. If he was stupid enough to think a relationship might work he'd only have egg on his face later. Libby would move onward and upward, while he struggled to keep up until eventually one of them decided there was too much distance between them.

"I have to wait…for the right time."

"It's now. Promise me you won't let this go to waste."

He drew a long deep breath. "Ma…"

"She's not Sadie, so if that's what you're worried about—"

"It's not."

"Then take the plunge. Don't be afraid."

Blood rushed in his ears, his body rebelling against her words. But what could he do? He couldn't blow his cover now. Not only would it make him look like a fool in front of his family but it would take away from Des and Gracie…they didn't deserve to have a shadow hang over their wedding because he was such a fuckup.

"Okay."

"I want you to know how proud I am of you." She pressed the velvet box into his hands. "Des told me about the idea you had for the cocktail classes at the bar. It sounds like a great idea."

"He did?" Paul turned the ring box over in his hand. He hadn't taken the business plan to Des yet, since there were a few final tweaks he wanted to make—Libby had taught him that much. If something was worth doing, it was worth doing properly.

"He was worried that he was too hard on you about the plans, but that must be a family trait. Right?"

"Yeah, we're a bunch of hard-asses."

"You're going to do great things, my son." She squeezed

him. "Now make sure you drive safely. I don't want any of the boxes getting broken because you're driving like a maniac."

"Good to see we're back to normal." He shook his head and pocketed the ring box.

A fake relationship had seemed so easy when he'd first suggested it to Libby. A few little lies, what harm could they do? But now he knew. He was in a world of guilt because he'd been a bad son. A bad brother.

A liar.

He swallowed as he climbed into the driver's seat and slammed the car door shut with a bang. He couldn't change the past, but he could make damn sure that after this was all done he'd be a new person. A better person.

Someone they'd be proud of for all the right reasons.

The hour and a half drive to the Yarra Valley hadn't done anything to improve Libby's mood. The neat rows of grapevines, greenery as far as the eye could see, and fluffy white marshmallow clouds blurred by, unappreciated, until the GPS announced she'd arrived at her destination.

She'd managed to avoid seeing anyone while she checked in. As she entered the room she was to share with Paul, the dark cloud remained firmly in place. Her father tended to have that effect on her.

Sinking down onto the massive king-size bed in the vineyard's hotel room, she brushed her hands over the luxurious covers. Tomorrow she'd have to face Paul's family again and front up to the web of lies she'd created. Including pretending to be Paul's fiancée.

"What the hell have I done?" she muttered into her hands.

"You won't find any answers there." Paul's voice caught her attention and she looked up.

"When did you get in?" She brushed her hands down the front of her dress and tried to ignore the flutter in her stomach.

He wore a suit. Sharp. Black. A white shirt opened at the collar to reveal tanned skin, and his shoes were polished to a high shine. His dark hair had been cut short since she saw him last, but the natural curl still showed through.

"You can close that pretty mouth of yours. Yes, I do own a suit." He smirked. "I got in early to have a meeting with the bridal party and the emcee."

"Oh." She nodded, pushing up from the bed and resting a hand on her suitcase. "I didn't realize there'd only be one bed here."

All the wedding guests were staying at the vineyard's accommodation, an old homestead that had been renovated and transformed into a luxury hotel. Gracie's mother knew the owner and the family had been given rooms with views of the Yarra Valley's sweeping landscape. The sun dipped low in the sky, casting ethereal gold light across the rolling hills.

The view could not have been more beautiful even if it had been perfected by an artist's brush.

"We're supposed to be a couple." Paul shrugged out of his jacket, and Libby allowed herself a single second to admire his broad shoulders before she spun around, pretending to inspect the room service menu. "A couple who's engaged, no less."

"Right." She swallowed.

How would she survive the night sleeping in the same bed as Paul? If she managed to keep her hands off him—which was unlikely—she wouldn't get a wink of sleep. If she gave in to the magnetic pull then there was a high chance of her being completely unable to keep her wits about her at the wedding.

That's what he did to her. One look, one touch, was all she needed to forget why she was here. Forget why she stayed away from relationships. Forget how much she'd let people hurt her in the past. Hell, if he kissed her hard enough she'd probably forget her own name.

But her father's visit had reminded her why the happily-ever-after endings of Hollywood movies were a sham.

"I can sleep on the couch," he said, snapping her attention back to the present. "You take the bed. I couldn't exactly ask for a room with two beds."

"No one would believe you were the waiting kind," she said attempting to lighten the mood, but a dark shadow passed over his face. "Not after the way you kissed me at your parents' place."

He nodded. "That was a hell of a kiss."

Talking about *that* would not help her state of mind, either.

"What do we need to do for the rehearsal dinner?" Libby grabbed her suitcase and lifted it onto the bed so she could unpack.

"Nothing. I have to give a speech, but you can just enjoy the wine and be your lovely self." He dropped down onto the bed and watched as she meticulously removed the items from her suitcase.

The tissue surrounding her wedding outfit crunched as

she lifted it out and unwrapped it. The black silk gleamed. It was so glossy it appeared wet in the dying light. For a moment she regretted not going with the safe option.

Hunger flared in Paul's face, his eyes fixated on her as she unfolded the silk to show its full glory. "I have a feeling I'm going to like that dress."

Libby said nothing as she reached for a hanger, slipping the shoulders over it and setting it up to hang from the wardrobe door so any creases could fall out. She placed her shoes down on the floor next to it.

"Is everything okay?" He narrowed his eyes at her as she continued to unpack.

For a moment she contemplated spilling it all, telling Paul about her father and the seeds of doubt he'd planted in her mind. But Paul wouldn't understand—his family was so warm and welcoming and kind. They loved one another too much to do the damage her father had done to her—well, except for Sadie and the other woman at the bridal shower.

Besides, she'd resolved her desire to stay relationship-free. She liked Paul. Too much. That was precisely why she needed to put some barriers in place.

"I'm fine. It's been a long week. I spent a lot of time meeting with restaurants." She forced a bright smile. "The press release I put out with a quote from your brother has done good things. Business is picking up again."

"That's great news." Paul nodded. "You should be really proud of yourself."

The words—intended to help, she was sure—turned in her stomach like sour milk. Should she be proud? What had her father said…cheap toxic cordial?

"I am," she said, hoping the words sounded truer than

they felt. "I'm grateful to both you and Des for helping me."

"I don't mind lending a hand, Tiger." He walked over to where his jacket hung over the back of a chair and stuck his hand into one of the pockets. "Especially not now that we're engaged."

She opened her mouth to fire off a comeback but the words evaporated on her tongue as he held out a small velvet box.

"I guess I should do this properly." He dropped down to one knee. "Libby Harris, will you do me the honor of pretending to marry me?"

A ring sparkled amongst the plush velvet cushions of the box. The ring wasn't traditional in any way. Teardrop diamonds criss-crossed the band like leaves in a wreath. Between the diamonds small rubies gleamed like berries.

While Libby froze, Paul stood and clasped her hand, sliding the ring onto her finger. Her whole body sparked like she was the center of an electrical storm. The room shifted around her as blood rushed to her head.

For a moment she could see the future. Waking up in the morning to Paul's hands on her body, his lips whispering in her ear the words she'd longed to hear all her life: *I love you, you belong.* Except she, like her mother, had heard those words before. How long would it be before he got bored, before he strayed? Before she wasn't good enough anymore?

"The ring belongs to my family," he said, running the pad of his thumb across her knuckles. "But it reminded me of you for some reason."

She wanted to believe him, but words meant nothing. Promises meant nothing. Her parents had told her they loved her as a child, but when was the last time she'd heard those words without them being attached to manipulation?

Paul steeled himself against the shock on Libby's face. Her hazel eyes widened as she gaped at the ring on her hand. The ring he'd slipped on as reverently as if it had actually meant something.

What the hell are you doing? Stop treating this like a real engagement. You're freaking her out!

"Are we really doing this?" she asked, her eyes never moving from the band on her finger.

It fit perfectly. Somehow he'd known it would.

"As predicted, Mum told every living relative and most of our neighbors that I popped the question."

Libby cringed. "I still can't believe I did that."

"Believe it. I've been fending off calls all week." He took a step back and dragged his eyes away from her hand.

"And after the wedding?" She looked up, her face pale. Drawn.

He shrugged. "We'll cross that bridge when we come to it."

Her head bobbed slowly. Her hand remained outstretched as though she wasn't ready to accept that the ring was part of her. The message couldn't have been clearer than if she'd carved it into a wall with a knife.

This relationship is as fake now as it was on day one.

"Paul…"

He forced his shoulders down and his breath to come out evenly. "Yeah?"

"I'm sorry I've messed everything up."

"It's fine. We'll deal with it." He waved her concern away and lifted his jacket from the chair, shrugging it on, one arm at a time. "I'll see you at dinner. Okay?"

She nodded at the ground.

Paul left the hotel room so quickly it must have looked as though a ghost had chased him out. He followed the line of the hallway, finding his family already gathered in the reception area where they were waiting to make their way as a group to the wedding chapel.

"Nervous?" he asked Gracie, who beamed up at him with a smile that could have lit an entire city.

"Not even a little bit." Her dark eyes sparkled.

Gracie's older sister stood next to her and held her hand. "This is such a special day. I'm so happy for you both."

"Don't start crying." Gracie swatted her. "You'll set me off."

Paul gave his soon-to-be sister-in-law a quick hug and went off in search of his mother. She had already started walking toward the chapel, and Paul fell into step beside her.

"Did you give her the ring?" she asked, looking up at him, her dark eyes filled with unstoppable excitement. "Where is she?"

"She doesn't need to be here for the rehearsal. You'll see her at dinner." They approached the chapel door, and Paul held it open for the others.

"I'm so proud of my boys," his mother said, shuffling past him.

"You just want grandkids," he called out after her and she laughed, nodding.

Yep, he'd dug himself a hole the size of a continent. A hole that would be awfully dark and lonely without Libby.

Chapter Thirteen

By the time the rehearsal concluded, Paul was itching to make a break for it. He needed food and space, not necessarily in that order.

Gracie's mother discussed something intently with the wedding planner while the bridal party and his parents stood around waiting. Her foot tapped a maddening beat against the floor as Gracie tried to smooth down the tension between the two women.

"If I ever get hitched I'm eloping to Vegas," Noah said, nodding toward the women. "No mother-in-law allowed."

"You want to get married?" Paul regarded his friend closely.

Noah shrugged and rubbed the stubble on his jaw. "I'm talking hypothetically. It'll never happen. Now you, on the other hand. You said weddings were stupid."

"Not you, too. Seriously, did she tell everyone?" He shook his head. "Besides, I believe I said tiny food was stupid."

"So it'll be burgers and fries at the union of Paul Chapman and Libby…?"

"Harris." He swallowed past a lump in his throat. "Libby Harris."

"I'm happy for you man. She's smart…well, except for her decision to date you." He slapped Paul on the back. "I had a chat with her when she came in to help Des set up for the tasting. Not sure how you managed to snag such a great girl."

"I have no idea." He shook his head.

They filtered out of the chapel and made their way to the restaurant. Libby was nowhere in sight, but her name was written in looping cursive on the place card next to his seat at the table. He looked at the empty chair.

"Were you worried I wouldn't show?" She materialized beside him as if conjured straight from his deepest, darkest desires.

Her hair was swept on top of her head, a few strands falling out to delicately frame her face. She'd changed out of jeans into a sleek black skirt and a silky emerald green top.

"Why do you say that?"

She shrugged and slipped her hand into his. The ring brushed against him as he interlaced his fingers with hers. "You were staring at the empty spot."

"Just wondering if they'd let me have your meal if you didn't show. I'm starving." He brushed him thumb over the ring, feeling the ridges of the setting as if memorizing them.

"No way. I'm going to eat every last bite."

Libby stepped closer to him as his mother rushed over proclaiming that she just *had* to see how the ring looked on her. Her grip tightened, her arm pressing into his side. For now, they were in this together.

He had twenty-four hours to decide what to do.

Having Paul's family fuss over her was a strange sensation. For some reason it reminded Libby of the time she'd been "invited" into the cool crowd at boarding school only to later find out it had all been a joke. She remembered crying over the lost sense of belonging, fleeting as it had been.

Only this time she knew it was a sham up front.

She toyed with the ring, twisting it around her finger until she was sure she'd worn a groove into her skin. The more people fussed, the closer she'd pressed against Paul. His arm around her was the only thing stopping her from running away, her promise to him the only thing holding her together.

Watching the two families laugh and celebrate was a surreal experience. They included her, brought her into the conversation, explained the jokes, and allowed her a peek into the thing she'd never have. A real family.

How would she ever be able to give this up?

Even Gracie's mother, who had a reputation as a bit of a control freak, seemed relaxed and was having a lively discussion with Paul's father. If Libby's father attended an event like this he would spend most of the evening complaining about the food and acting too important to partake in the conversation.

The very thought of her father made Libby's throat

clench. Why couldn't he love her the way she was? Why couldn't he be proud of her?

The waiters arrived at the table carrying dessert in an alternate drop. Chocolate mousse with raspberries and a heavenly slice of baked cheesecake. Too bad her appetite had been whittled away by the bad taste left in her mouth from that afternoon.

"Don't you like mousse?" Paul touched her leg under the table. "We can swap if you like. I'm not fussy when it comes to dessert."

She shook her head. "I love mousse."

"Then why are you looking at it like it's the spawn of the devil?"

"Dad came to see me today," she blurted out, unable to carry the weight of that burden by herself.

"Ahh." Paul put his fork down and turned to her. "Tell me what happened."

"I know there's no point rehashing it—he'll never change." She toyed with the ornate desert spoon, scooping out a miniscule amount and letting herself have a taste. "But he makes me so…so…"

"Speechless?" he offered with a gentle squeeze of his hand.

Despite herself, Libby smiled. "Ashamed."

"Why ashamed?"

"Nothing I do is good enough. He never fails to make me feel like I'm *this* big." She gestured with a small space between her fingers. "I'm like a failed experiment that he's desperately trying to get back on track. I wish he'd leave me be."

"No you don't." Paul's dark eyes cut through her, seeing

the truth that she tried so hard to keep hidden.

The little girl who'd only ever wanted to be loved by her family.

"You want him to accept you," he continued. "That's why it hurts when he speaks to you like that. If you really wanted him to leave you be then you'd simply avoid him."

She blinked. "Well, look at you, Sigmund Freud."

"Not just a pretty face." He winked and slung an arm around her shoulder, the tips of his fingers tracing a pattern at the edge of her sleeve. "I know a thing or two about difficult families."

"You don't know how lucky you are. At least your parents love you."

"I'm sure yours do, too. If your father really thought you were a failure do you think he'd keep trying?"

"Well…no," she admitted. She'd seen her father cut ties with people he'd deemed not worth his time, and he'd done it without a backward glance. "But he's trying to make me fit into his life plan."

"Yeah, because he thinks he knows what's best."

She huffed. "He doesn't. He said I'm wasting my life."

"Have you ever sat him down and explained why you want to work for yourself? What it means to you?"

Of course she hadn't, she'd decided to "stick it to the man" by putting her studies on hold without telling him and then she'd gone and done her own thing. She'd always done her own thing…that's what you did if you were alone.

She valued her independence even if it was borne out of loneliness.

"I take that as a no." Paul pressed his cheek to the top of her head.

She turned, her face tucked in to the crook of his neck, the scent of aftershave on his skin kicking up memories of them together, of his hands on her. Of the way he made her feel wanted, desired. Whole.

"You think I should talk to him?"

He nodded. "It's worth a shot. What's the worst that can happen? He still doesn't agree with you, and you're no worse off than you are now."

She swallowed, already dreading the conversation. But Paul was right, her sudden rebellion must have come as a huge surprise to her father since she'd been so obedient her whole life. She hadn't taken him through her business plan or told him her long-term goals. He didn't know about the charity she hoped to set up once her business was stable, nor the volunteer work she'd signed up for at the local community center.

Her business might not seem as important as his career as a surgeon. In reality, it probably wasn't. She wasn't saving lives, but she *would* make a difference to the women she worked with, the ones she'd eventually employ when the company grew. The ones she'd teach and nurture in her volunteer work.

"Thank you," she said, sitting up and dunking her spoon into the mousse.

A warm smile spread across his lips. "You're very welcome. I'm glad to see the appetite is back."

She nodded. "This is amazing."

Beside her, Paul shifted in his seat. He pulled a set of white index cards out of his jacket pocket and tapped them against his thigh, bouncing his leg in a steady rhythm.

"Is it speech time now?" she asked, trying to peek at his

scratchy handwriting.

He pressed the cards between his hands, hiding the words from her. "Almost."

"I thought best man speeches were only a duty for the big day."

He looked at her from the corner of his eye. "I'm giving a speech then, too, but this is something just for the immediate family. Don't worry, I'll be wheeling out all the embarrassing tales of Des's childhood tomorrow."

"How far back did you have to go to get any dirt on him?"

Paul crinkled his nose. "Too far. He's always been the more serious brother. But there *is* a story about a disastrous tattooing incident."

She took a sip of her champagne, grateful for the diversion from her inner turmoil. "Do tell."

"You'll have to wait till tomorrow like everyone else. You don't get privileges just 'cause I put a ring on it." He leaned in and nipped at her earlobe before planting a kiss on her cheek.

Libby caught Des and his mother watching them, their heads turning back to each other when she caught their eye. Leone looked so happy she might spontaneously combust. Had Paul kissed her because she was looking? Libby couldn't tell what was real and what was for show anymore.

Swallowing her unease, she smiled at Paul just as a blissfully happy fiancée would...or at least how she imagined one would. "What's this speech about?"

"You'll see." His face turned serious, the playful sparkle in his eyes replaced by an unreadable blankness. "Listen carefully, though."

What on earth was that supposed to mean? Before

she could ask, Paul stood and held the cards loosely in one hand. He looked powerful and handsome in his suit, the cut making his broad shoulders look even more imposing and his slim waist even more defined. Though with a body like his you could dress him in a paper bag, and he'd still look incredible.

"My brother has asked me to say a few words tonight," Paul started. "But first I'd like to raise a toast to Des and Gracie. May tomorrow be everything you hoped for and more."

Warmth spread through Libby's chest as she watched Paul toasting his brother and soon-to-be sister-in-law. When it came to crunch time, Paul was every bit the kind of man she'd once hoped to end up with. Kind, articulate, sexy. Most of all, he'd never tried to change a thing about her.

"With all the jokes and embarrassing stories I've saved for tomorrow I really didn't have much material left for this speech. So I got a little philosophical." Paul winked at Des.

"Here we go," Des said with a chuckle. "Just remember who'll be giving the speech at your wedding one day."

"I thought about the ideal relationship and the kind of qualities one might need to have a happy marriage. Now, I'm no expert as you know." Paul took a sip of his drink and placed it back down on the table. "I know some people have a bit of a wish list when it comes to the ideal partner."

Some eyes at the table turned to Gracie, who flushed and waved them away. "I've changed, I promise!"

"A lot of people say they want a partner who's funny, intelligent, good-looking, rich. All of those things are great, but a true partnership requires something more." He stole a glance at Libby. "For a relationship to last you need someone who's going to inspire you. Someone who's going to push you, change you for the better, and challenge you. When that person comes into your life you'll question everything...including your sanity."

The table tittered, but Libby couldn't drag her eyes away from Paul. Had he reached into her mind and plucked those very thoughts from her head? He made *her* question everything she believed about family and relationships. He pushed her and challenged her to think creatively, to solve problems without getting stressed out...even when she'd blurted out the lie about them getting married. He was her opposite in the best way possible.

"If you can wake every day beside the same person and say that you still feel inspired a year, ten years, fifty years from now," he paused, his eyes flicking down to Libby for the briefest second. "Then that's the best possible thing you can ask for."

He continued the speech, citing some funny moments in Gracie and Des's relationship, but Libby's head swam, blocking out the anecdotes and laughter at the table. She'd never been anyone's inspiration before. Hell, she'd never been anything but a temporary situation to the people in her life...aside from Nina. She'd been a temporary child until her mother had one she planned for, a temporary daughter to her father who wanted a carbon copy of himself, a temporary girlfriend to her ex until he grew tired of her.

As Paul finished his speech Libby clapped so hard her palms stung. "That was beautiful."

He shrugged. "Just doing my job."

Was that all it was? Sweet words for the sake of his family? Libby knew one thing for certain, she needed to know how Paul felt. How he *really* felt underneath the fake engagement and the layer of emotional protection he'd built.

She *would* find out before this wedding was over.

Paul plied himself with alcohol after the speech. The words hadn't seemed so raw when he'd written them in haste, shocked by how cathartic it felt to get all that crap out of his head and onto a page.

He'd also needed a few beers in him to distract himself from Libby and the way she watched him like a hawk. Had the speech freaked her out? Probably. Did he care? No. They were out in the open now and, if she questioned him, then he'd use Gracie and Des as an excuse.

Before meeting Libby he would *never* have given a speech like that, but being with her had made him appreciate how good he had it. His family wasn't perfect by any stretch, but they were his.

"That dessert was amazing," Libby said as the waiters came to clear the last plates. "I'm not going to fit into my dress tomorrow."

"I am! I don't care if it takes five people to stuff me into the damn thing." Gracie chuckled. "There's so much boning in the corset I may not be able to breathe, anyway."

The girls hugged as the guests parted ways, and Libby looped her arm through Paul's. She wobbled on her heels as they made their way back to the room.

"Have a bit to drink, did you?" he asked.

She moaned. "They kept topping up my glass so I have no idea how much I had. If I have a hangover tomorrow just kill me and put me out of my misery."

"You won't be much use to me then." Electricity sizzled along his arm where she held onto him for support.

"I'm not much use to anyone," she muttered.

They arrived at the hotel room and Paul held Libby up with one arm while he opened the door. "Why would you say that?"

"Didn't you hear what I said before?" She spat the words out, her features twisted. "He said I'm *wasting* my life."

"Yes, and you agreed to talk to him. That doesn't change because you've had a few drinks."

Libby tripped on the carpet, and Paul steadied her before scooping her up into his arms and kicking the door closed behind them.

"You don't need to carry me," she said, wriggling in his grip.

"Since you can't even walk through a doorway in your current state…yes, I do." He set her down on the edge of the bed and caught a foot in his hand, fiddling with the buckle at her ankle. "Why do you have to wear these damn fiddly shoes?"

"They're pretty." She flopped back and flung an arm over her eyes. "Tell the room to stop spinning."

"You'll be all right. I'll get you a glass of water once you're out of the shoes." He handled her as gently as he could when her body hung like a ragdoll over the edge of the bed.

By the time he'd returned with her water, Libby had stripped and crawled into bed. Her naked body was mostly covered by the thick white sheet, but his mind knew exactly how to fill in the blanks. He knew how smooth and soft her thighs felt, how she had a smattering of light freckles all over her body, how her nipples were perfectly rosy and responsive.

"Here." He helped her to sit up and handed her the water. "Drink it slowly."

She sipped, holding the glass in one hand and the sheet with her other hand. "I don't want you to sleep on the couch tonight."

"You're drunk," he pointed out.

"Tipsy," she corrected. "I know exactly what I'm doing."

"That's what I'm afraid of," he muttered.

For someone who pulled sex off the table at the outset, she'd certainly done a one-eighty. Not that he was complaining, but the idea of sex with her now felt loaded. Dangerous.

Who the hell are you anymore?

"Good night." He pressed his lips to her forehead and stood, shrugging out of his jacket. "Make sure you drink plenty of water."

Her still made-up eyes had fluttered closed, her features softened. He'd always scoffed at those who referred to people as angels when they slept, but Libby may as well have been wrapped up in big golden wings.

He snapped the light off and undressed in the dark. The bed squeaked as Libby shifted and he made his way to the couch.

You're turning into a sap, Chapman. Get your head out of the clouds and back to reality—this is not *a relationship.*

Chapter Fourteen

Paul's eyes opened but no light greeted him. He blinked, trying to adjust to the darkness while wondering why the hell he was awake. His neck ached from where he'd fallen asleep at a strange angle on the couch, the throw cushion acting as his pillow nowhere to be found.

He pushed up into a sitting position and kneaded the knot in his neck. Perhaps he should have taken Libby up on her offer to share the bed.

The sound of a door closing caught his attention, then a thin beam of light filtered out from under the bathroom door. He must have heard Libby getting out of bed. Strange, since his family joked that he could easily sleep through a monster truck rally.

He walked over to the bathroom as she opened the door with a fresh glass of water in her hand.

"How are you feeling?"

"Oh!" She shook her head. "You startled me."

The bathroom light fell into the room, outlining the curves of her silhouette and catching the red-gold edges of her hair. She'd thrown on a T-shirt at some point and it came down to the tops of her thighs, leaving miles of shapely legs exposed.

"I'm fine." She sipped her water and leaned against the doorframe. "I've got a bit of a headache, but otherwise I'm good as new."

Her eyes skimmed over him, catching on the only item of clothing he wore—a pair of boxer briefs. Shadows obscured her face, but nothing could hide the sharp intake of her breath in the silent room.

"You should get back to bed," he said, swallowing against the flood of desire that raged in him. He burned from the inside out, his skin begging to have her hands on him.

"You should come with me."

"Libby," he warned. "I don't want to take advantage of you."

"I wish you would." She stepped closer and touched her palm to his bare chest. "I'm not drunk, and I'm perfectly capable of voicing what I want."

He took the glass from her hand and guided her back to the bed. "What do you want, Tiger?"

She dropped down to the mattress, pulling him with her until he knelt over her, nudging her thighs apart with his knees. "To pretend we're not pretending…just for tonight."

Before he could protest she looped her arms around his neck and dragged his head down to hers. He feasted on her mouth, greedily seeking out her tongue, sucking on her lower lip and dragging it between his teeth. Nothing about this was pretend.

"Libby." He pulled his head back, trying to think through the fog of arousal that engulfed him. "We can't—"

"Shhh." She pressed a finger to his lips

He buried his face in her neck, feeling the flutter of her pulse against his lips. His hand caught the hem of her T-shirt and dragged it up, exposing her pale skin to the moonlight. Heat flared within him like a fire blazing out of control. She fanned him. Heightened his senses. Filled him with burning power.

Tossing the T-shirt over the side of the bed, he brought his head down to one breast. Above him, her soft moan made a tremor run down his spine. She fisted her hand in his hair and arched against him.

"Let's go slow and enjoy it." He moved to the other breast, lavishing attention on the nipple with his tongue.

"I lose control with you." She ran her hands over his shoulders and scraped her nails along his skin.

"Me too."

He kissed his way down the plane of her belly, relishing the feel of her soft skin against his lips. Something told him that tonight was his last chance to hold her in his arms before reality came crushing down on them both in the morning. So he would pretend, as she'd asked, and deal with the fallout tomorrow.

He pressed his lips to the inside of her thigh, skirting around her heat. Making her wait. Drawing out the moment that they would drown together.

When he moved his mouth to her sex, she cried out and the sound shattered something inside him. He couldn't wait, didn't want to. Every second with Libby was a precious gift that would soon expire. He focused on her center, feeling the quake in her thighs, pushing her higher and higher until she broke.

A shudder ran through her as she came, his name falling from her lips over and over. As she floated back down he pressed his cheek to her belly, and she ran her fingers through his hair.

"You're so very good at that," she said, the fog of climax blending her words together.

Her skin was smooth against him, her warmth fueling his desire. He pushed up onto his hands and hovered over her. A smile pulled at her lips, her eyes heavy-lidded. Sooty lashes touched as she blinked and he drank it all in, committing every curve, every line, every plane to his memory.

"Are you just going to stare at me?" she asked with a husky laugh.

"For starters." He ran a palm over her ribcage and caught the weight of her breast in one hand, smoothing his thumb over her nipple.

She hummed in pleasure. "And then?"

"Everything." He came down onto her, resting on one arm so he could brush the hair from her face with his free hand. "I want every moan, every shudder, every orgasm I can possibly get from you."

"Greedy." She kissed his shoulder.

"I am when it comes to you." The weight of his words should have driven him away but instead it seemed to suck the air from between them until there was nothing but skin on skin, their hearts aligned.

When he pushed inside her the whole world slipped away. Wrapping his arms around her waist, he pulled back until he was sitting upright and she straddled him. Her hips moved up and down, the rhythm perfectly matched as he slanted his mouth over hers. She tasted sweet and warm and familiar. Like home. Like everything he'd once wanted.

"I don't regret this," she whispered, her lips brushing against his ear. "I don't regret being with you."

"Me neither, Tiger." He stroked her face with one hand and ran a thumb along her lower lip.

He reached down between them and found her sweet spot, feeling the tremors run through her as he stroked, intent on having her come around him. She tightened, her forehead dropping down to his shoulder, allowing him to fully support her.

"Paul, I…" she gasped. "I…"

"Let it happen." He kissed her forehead, her cheekbone, her temple. "Let me feel you."

Her teeth sank into his shoulder and she muffled the sharp cry of release as she tipped over. He buried himself deep inside her and lost himself to the sensation of her pleasure, giving up control to feel her as he came.

His arms were wrapped around her so tightly that no air could pass between them. They were fused together, her body wrapped around his, heels digging into his back. He cradled her as he lowered them back to the mattress, her hands never letting go.

The words from his speech came echoing back to him. He questioned everything with Libby curled in his arms, and his sanity was high on that list.

L ibby woke the next morning to the gentle pressure of lips on her skin. Exhausted from a night of too much pleasure and too little sleep, she tried unsuccessfully to clear the fog away.

"Don't get up," Paul said as he stroked the hair out of her face. "I have to go, but you don't need to get down there for another few hours. Order room service and stay in bed."

She smiled, blinking to bring his face into focus. "I wish you could stay."

"You won't be thinking that when you starfish on that bed." His lips brushed against hers.

He'd already changed into his tux, and he smelled of soap and cologne. Combined with his olive skin and dark hair, he looked as though he'd stepped from a magazine ad. But the hunger in her eyes reminded her that he wasn't just a handsome face; he was a protective, caring, passionate man whom she'd fallen in love with.

Her heart thumped as the words swirled in her mind. *Love*? Did she really love Paul?

"You need some rest. I think I wore you out last night." He chuckled and looked around for his phone, slipping it into the inside pocket of his jacket.

"We wore each other out." She pulled the covers up to her chin, as though a few layers of cotton could protect her from the weight of her realization.

"Very true. I've got to go, but I'm looking forward to seeing you in that black dress." He leaned against the door as though he didn't want to leave.

"Are you looking forward to getting me out of it?" The thought left her breathless and, despite the fact that they'd made love not a few hours before, her body already ached for him again.

She'd become addicted to him, his touch inciting a hunger and craving that was totally new to her. But it wasn't only about sexual fulfilment…he made her whole. All the doubts and insecurities her family had fostered in her vanished when he was there. He filled the grooves in her soul, soothed her wounds, smoothed out the rough parts of her.

The end had come too soon, and she didn't want it to be over. Ever.

"Do you need to ask me that?" He waggled his brows and opened the door, hovering for a moment before leaving her alone.

Libby stared up at the ceiling, her eyes refusing to focus. Her body still tingled with the memory of his hands and lips on her, as though he'd tattooed the feeling onto her skin.

As she raised her hand to cover her face she noticed the band of diamonds on her ring finger. She'd forgotten to take it off before she went to bed, and now the diamonds glistened like tears catching sunlight.

What happened to avoiding relationships? Did she really want to put herself out there and risk the shame and rejection that had plagued her for her entire twenty-five years?

Yes.

Her mind may try to argue, but her heart spoke the truth. It sang the word from the deepest part of her soul.

She loved Paul Chapman, her fake boyfriend turned fake fiancé. All she had to do was tell him…and hope that what they'd shared hadn't all been in her head. She couldn't have imagined the looks he gave her during the speech last night, nor the way he seemed drawn to her the way she was drawn to him.

The black dress hung from the wardrobe door, a silent challenge. It would be easy to stay warm and cozy inside her comfort zone, but there was nothing there for her anymore.

She'd taken a risk starting Libby Gal Cocktails, and it was starting to pay off. Perhaps if she took that same risk on love she'd find happiness there, too.

Libby sat up and swung her legs out of the bed. Today would be the day she let her heart do the talking, and she'd have an answer one way or another.

B y the time the reception was due to start Paul had decided that perhaps weddings weren't so bad. His mother had turned into a weepy mess in the room where the family had a quiet breakfast, but everything else had been fairly painless.

Paul, Des, and Noah had shared a celebratory Scotch with his father in the dressing room. Despite his outwardly confident demeanor, Paul knew his brother was anxious for the proceedings to kick off.

The chapel had been decorated, and the boys stood in their places in front of the neat rows of pews that would soon be filled with family and friends. Music floated through the air as people filtered in, sorting themselves on either the bride or groom's side.

"You ready?" Paul asked, though he'd never seen anyone so ready to get married before.

"One hundred percent." Des grinned. "I wish Mum would stop the water works, though."

"Not going to happen." Noah shook his head. "Not a hope in hell."

Paul chuckled and adjusted his cuffs. "She's already naming her grandchildren, you know that, right?"

"Hopefully she won't have to wait too long." Des clasped his hands behind his back and surveyed the chapel. "Then it's your turn."

"We're focusing on you today," Paul reminded him.

"I'm happy for you. You deserve it."

Paul swallowed and pretended to fix a cufflink. Did he, really? Libby was this incredible creature, creative, a risk taker. She blew him away every time they made love.

Made love.

He hadn't thought about sex in such a way since...forever. The collar on his shirt felt too tight, like hands closing in on his windpipe. He bounced on the balls of his feet and kept his eyes straight ahead.

Then Libby walked through the door, and the rest of the room fell away. Black fabric swished against her skin, the modest hem length and sleeves contrasted by the flash of bare back she exposed when she turned to greet the usher and grab a copy of the program.

Red hair gleamed as it tumbled over one shoulder, tied loosely with a black ribbon. She caught his eye and broke into a bright smile. Following the line of people heading down the aisle she slipped into a pew on the groom's side.

How would he pay attention during the ceremony with her sitting right there?

"Paul?" Des tapped him on the shoulder. "I asked if you had the rings. Don't freak me out, man."

"Right here." He patted his breast pocket. "I wouldn't forget the most important part of the show."

"Second most important," Des said, turning to look down the aisle as the organ music started.

Chapter Fifteen

The wedding sped by, time seemed to zoom ahead as his brother took the biggest leap of his life. A twinge of envy had replaced the disdain that colored Paul's life almost two months ago when Gracie and Des first announced their date.

He didn't have the opportunity to talk to Libby as they were whisked away for photos right after the ceremony—to catch the right light, according to the photographer. Then the guests were ushered into the reception area in time for the emcee to announce the bridal party and newly married couple.

He milled around outside, enjoying the afternoon sunlight and cool breeze carrying the scents of greenery and wine. Laughter and conversation floated from within the venue—an old barn that had been converted into a luxury ballroom—and Paul shoved his hands into his pockets. He'd been anxious to talk to Libby from the moment she'd stepped into the chapel, and the itching feeling to be near her grew stronger with each moment that passed.

"Paul?" A feminine voice caught his attention and made the hairs on his neck stand up.

He'd know her voice anywhere. Sadie. He turned slowly, drawing back his shoulders and unclenching his hands.

"I think all the wedding guests should be inside by now," he said coolly. "Are you lost?"

She shook her head, neat blond hair swishing about her face. Her hand rested over a small bump at her belly, floral fabric skimming over her new shape, almost concealing it. As always, she looked elegant and put-together. Sadie never had a hair out of place, never looked flustered or over-whelmed or stressed.

"I'm not lost. I hoped to catch you for a moment so we could talk in private." Dark smudges under her eyes were barely concealed with makeup.

He forced himself not to have any sympathy for her. "I have nothing to say."

"But I do." She shifted her weight and, when he didn't respond, she continued. "I realized that I never apologized for walking out on you."

"Or for cheating on me," he pointed out, looking around to make sure he hadn't missed the call for the introductions.

"I'm truly sorry," she said, her eyes bright. "You never deserved that."

A bird chirped overhead. Sunlight filtered down through tall trees. This was far too picturesque a place to be opening up old wounds.

"No one deserves that."

"I feel like I should explain," she pressed on. "We never

talked about it, and I know you must hate me, but I had my reasons."

"Why do you feel the need to say something now, in the middle of a bloody wedding of all times?"

"I don't want to become a mother with something like this hanging over me, and I know that you'd never talk to me unless we were forced to be in the same room." She looked down at her stomach. "How can I teach my children to be good people when I did something like that and never apologized or explained myself?"

Her fine brows knitted, and she looked at him with such despair that he couldn't help but soften. "Boy or girl?"

"One of each." She nodded slowly, as if convincing herself. "Talk about jumping in with two feet."

He shook his head. "I hope you're catching up on sleep now."

"You know I always loved my sleep." She glanced over at Paul's mother who quickly turned her head away as if she hadn't been trying to listen.

"You've got a few minutes before we get called in," he said, bracing himself. "Say what you need to say, because I don't ever want to talk about this again."

"Thank you." She wrung her hands in front of her. "I wanted you to know I never set out to cheat on you. I didn't plan it, it just…happened. I was lonely."

"Lonely?" He fought back the urge to argue. How could she have ever felt lonely?

They were in a relationship. Wasn't that the very opposite of being alone?

"Maybe that's the wrong word." She tucked her pale hair behind one ear. "Maybe isolated is a better choice."

"Doesn't sound much better to me," he said, his shoulders stiff and bunched beneath the tuxedo jacket.

"I wanted all these things out of life that you didn't. It frustrated me because I felt like I either had to forgo what I wanted or had to try and change you, which wasn't fair, either."

"What things?"

"Babies," she patted her stomach. "Marriage, career ambitions. I wanted a partner who could reach for the stars with me. I wasn't satisfied being alone at night while you worked in the bar, knowing that girls were hitting on you left, right, and center. How could we have ever raised a family like that?"

"I would have gotten a different job." He'd never actively thought about changing careers, since he felt so at home in the bar. But he knew if she'd given him a chance he would have traded it to have a family. "Why didn't you say something?"

"I tried to talk to you about it but you said I was worrying over nothing. My life was slipping away, and I couldn't do a thing about it."

He'd done that to her by not listening, by not being ambitious enough. It didn't excuse the cheating, *nothing* would excuse that. But he'd been a crappy boyfriend to her, apparently…and he hadn't even known it.

"I'm sorry I acted without breaking things off with you first." Tears swam in her eyes. "I wanted more, Paul. But I understood that you didn't. Sometimes I wish I'd been able to be happy with what we had…but I couldn't."

He sucked in a breath. "You didn't allow me a chance to give you more."

"I didn't want to change you, it's not who you are…and that's okay. Not everyone has to set the world alight."

The words cut him to the bone. Sadie had seen that she wouldn't be happy with him and so she'd jumped ship when something better came along. Her explanation not only didn't make him feel better about the way things ended, it made the pain *worse*. Before, he'd been able to blame her for doing the wrong thing but now he saw that she'd felt ignored, isolated. Uninspired…the very thing he'd cited in his speech as a key element to any relationship.

All because of him.

"Paul!" Des called out. "They're calling us in."

"Go." He motioned for Sadie to slip into the reception room before the bridal party entered.

"I wish I could take back what I did." She gathered the lengths of her dress in one hand and walked carefully along the cobblestone path. "I wish I'd ended things the right way. You deserved better than that. I really am sorry."

He nodded, a lump lodged so hard in his throat no words could pass. Sadie hovered for a moment, as though she wanted to say something else but then she ducked her head and entered the room without another word.

The emcee's booming voice announced that it was time to bring in the bridal party.

Time to put his game face on.

Libby stood by the side of the room, watching as the bridal party were called into the room. Paul walked with his head held high, Gracie's sister, Emmaline, on his arm. They looked every bit the glamorous couple with his dark looks and her shimmering silver gown.

Her belly twinged. Libby had never been the jealous sort, but seeing them together made her realize how much she wanted to be the one standing next to him. The thought of him ever being with another woman tore her up inside.

The room erupted in a raucous cheer when the bride and groom walked through the doors. Gracie's floor-length gown swirled around her legs. Her grin was only outdone by Des, who looked so happy he could take flight at any moment.

"Don't you love weddings?" Another wedding guest said to Libby as she settled against the wall next to her.

"They're very happy occasions." Libby nodded, smiling as Gracie and Des started doing the rounds with bridesmaids and groomsmen in tow.

"Are you from the groom's side or the bride's?" the blonde asked.

"The groom's. You?"

"Bride's. My mother and Gracie's mother go way back; they were determined for us to be friends ever since we were in kindergarten." She smiled. "I'm glad Gracie found someone like Des—he's good for her."

Libby nodded. "They make a great couple."

"I hear the brother is a bit of a wild one. A friend of mine always goes to their bar, and apparently he leaves with a different girl each week." She waggled her brows. "Maybe I'll get lucky."

Libby sucked in a breath and didn't say anything. She knew Paul had been that way once. The question was, had he changed? He felt something for her, she was sure of it…but whether or not he'd be able to admit it was something else.

"Lovely chatting with you," Libby said, with an over-bright smile. "I must go and find my boyf—fiancé."

The music had started, and waiters emerged from the kitchen carrying trays of smoked salmon hors d'oeuvres, tiny spoons of goat cheese and beet puree and, mercifully, large flutes of champagne.

Libby flagged down a waiter and grabbed a glass, taking a hearty sip before she went in search of Paul. She found him talking with Noah and another wedding guest.

"Hey," she said, smiling as she made her way up to him. "You did well in the ceremony."

"You mean I stood in my place and didn't say a word." He smirked. "Not exactly high brain-power activities there."

"You didn't roll your eyes at any point," she joked. "That would have taken a bit of effort."

Instead of making him laugh, which was the desired effect, he frowned. His jaw worked, the muscles tightening as though he were grinding his teeth. "What can I say, I'm a disciplined guy."

Libby sipped her champagne. "It was a beautiful wedding. I'm so happy for Gracie and Des."

He nodded, his eyes glancing over her shoulder. Butterflies fluttered in her stomach, and not the good kind. Something wasn't right, she could feel it in her bones.

"Why don't we have a dance?" She grabbed his hand and tugged him toward the dance floor where everyone had already congregated.

Since Gracie and Des had decided to skip the formal "first dance" and instead had wanted everyone to share the moment with them, the emcee had called everyone to the floor. Gracie and Des danced hand-in-hand with the flower girl.

"Come on, it'll be fun," she cajoled, setting her champagne flute down on a high table.

"I would hate to disappoint my fiancée." Paul's face was hard as a mask of stone, his eyes closed off. Inaccessible.

They found a spot within the throng, and Libby pulled him close, wrapping her arms around his waist. He felt stiff in her grip, his hands landing lightly on her without any of his usual possessiveness. It was almost as if he didn't want to touch her.

"What's wrong? You seem a little…distracted."

"I guess I am. I also didn't get a lot of sleep last night." He looked at her properly for the first time since she'd walked over to him.

"Are you prepared for round two?" She ran her hands up and down his back, feeling the muscles tense beneath her touch.

"We'll see…I don't know when my best man duties finish up today."

His response couldn't have been more lukewarm if he'd tried. Had he gotten his fill and become bored? She pushed the worry away. She *knew* Paul; he wasn't the guy that others made him out to be.

"I was hoping we could talk," she said, mustering the courage she wished she had.

Fake it till you make it, right?

"Talk?" His eyes darted across her face. "What's there to talk about?"

"Us." The word came out shakier than she'd hoped, but she had to know how he felt. If he had any feelings for her beyond what they'd shared in bed.

"What about us?" His jaw tightened again. "What's wrong with what's going on now?"

"I didn't say anything was wrong." She shook her head, unsure what prompted his question. "Actually, I thought things were going pretty well."

"Yeah?" He glanced over her shoulder again as they danced.

"Don't you?" She cupped his jaw and gently turned his face back to hers.

"It's fine. I appreciate you holding up your end of the deal. I'm sure this is boring as hell for you."

She blinked. Where was the passionate man who'd made her see stars last night? Where was the man who had given her courage when her own father cut her down? He wasn't in her arms. That much was certain.

"Paul, I'm trying to tell you something." She sighed, tension coiling her body tight like a spring.

"Then spit it out."

She closed her eyes. "I love you."

"What?" He jerked in her arms, reeling back as if she'd slapped him.

The three words swirled in her mind as loud as a raging storm, but her heart couldn't put them out there again, not when he looked at her like that. "I had to say it. I need to know if…if you feel the same."

He stood stock-still in the middle of the bustling dance floor. Only when curious stares came from the other wedding guests did he step back into her arms, though she may as well have been holding a plank of wood.

"Libby, we agreed not to go down that path." He shook his head as if trying to shake her words away. "No emotions, right?"

"We said no sex, too, but you didn't seem to have a problem with that." Pain spiraled through her uncontrollably, her breath caught in her throat.

"Neither did you, if memory serves me correctly." His mouth set into a firm line, and he avoided her gaze. "I didn't force you into anything."

"Look me in the eye and tell me that you don't feel anything for me," she said. "I know I take risks, but they're not on a whim. I've *thought* about this, I've analyzed it."

Silence. They moved awkwardly to the music as she waited for his response.

"Answer me, Paul. Is this relationship totally fake?"

He let out a breath. "Yes."

Libby's eyes lowered, and she nodded slowly. The disappointment on her face scythed through him like a blade. He should never have crossed the line with her knowing he wouldn't be able to be the man she wanted.

Lying to her was torture, but it was for the best. She was a brilliant, intelligent, and passionate woman who deserved more than a bartender who failed so badly at relationships that he drove people away. Drove them toward other people. Deep down he knew Libby would never cheat on him the way Sadie had, but she would become unhappy and eventually leave. Knowing how much he felt for her now, before they'd even fully explored the potential of each other, would mean her leaving would kill him. Whether it happened in six months, a year, five years…he couldn't take it.

"Here I was thinking that your speech last night was about me. How naive is that?" She steeled herself, tilting her face up to his and setting her shoulders back.

"It's not naive."

"Yes, clearly it is. Because if it wasn't you'd be telling me the truth right now."

"The truth?"

"You *do* feel something for me, I know I didn't imagine it. But for some reason you're too frightened to admit it." Her cheeks were flushed, her eyes glimmering. "Or do you think you'll get bored only being with one woman?"

"You want the truth?" He struggled to stay calm amid the melange of emotions battling inside him. "I was ready to propose to Sadie. I'd picked out the ring, and I was going to lay myself on the line for her."

She didn't say anything, but he saw the flicker of her eyes, the softening of her lips. Pity. Empathy. Two things he neither wanted nor deserved.

"I would have given her everything, and it wouldn't have been enough. Now I know not to go down that path in the first place. I'm not cut out for relationships."

"But you are," she said, her eyes wide and pleading.

"Libby," he growled, the emotion he'd tried so hard to pack down bubbling up inside him like hot lava. "Don't."

She swallowed "Don't what?"

"Try to make me believe. I'm doing the right thing by both of us." He sighed. "I'm keeping us to our agreement."

"How very noble of you," she spat. "But it's complete crap. What you're actually doing is punishing me for her mistakes…and I deserve better than that."

The chatter and cheer of the crowd drowned out the rest

of her words, though there was no mistaking her feelings from the look on her face. Her eyes narrowed at him, the scrutiny making his skin itch.

What could he say? If he told the truth about how he felt she'd want to pursue it, to understand his feelings, to ask questions. All of those things would strip him back, make him vulnerable to her. Sadie was right, he didn't want what they wanted. Right now he wanted to protect them both from the future disappointment.

A squeal of a microphone cut through the air, and the emcee announced it was time for speeches. Before he knew what was happening, a cocktail was thrust into his hand: the pink Bellini made from Libby's vodka and his recipe. Their first creation as a team.

She looked at him, analyzing and cataloging his every movement. The glimmer of hope in her eyes slayed him. He'd extinguish that flame, like he had with Sadie.

"I have to go," he said touching her shoulder lightly. "It's speech time."

She flinched. "Go. I'll be ready to play happy fiancée when you get back. Enjoy it, because after this I'm outta here."

Better now than later.

Chapter Sixteen

The surface of the bar was smooth beneath his hands. Paul looked out over the restaurant, surveying the boxes displaying Libby's logo piled up on the tables. Tonight Libby Gal Cocktails had its official launch at First.

But he'd be gone before the first champagne cork popped.

It'd been a month since the wedding. Des had delayed the launch until he returned from his honeymoon to ensure he could endorse the product in person. He'd wanted to give Libby the best possible chance of exposure and, since the article in Gastronomy magazine had exploded, his word meant something in the industry.

A few days after Des had returned from Europe, Paul broke the news to him and the whole family. He and Libby had not only broken up, but they'd never really been engaged.

Spilling the whole truth had been her idea. It was the

single source of contact he'd had with her since the wedding. An email requesting he tell his family the truth so she could front up to Des and give him the option to back out. She said she'd wanted her business to succeed without lies.

His mother was devastated, and Des had been understandably angry. But he'd grown to like Libby enough to hash it out with her personally, and he hadn't spilled a word of their conversation to Paul.

You broke up with her for a reason, so move on. Stop thinking about her.

To keep his mind off the gaping hole Libby's absence made in his life, he'd thrown himself into setting up the mixology school. Business plans, budgets, and forecasts had become his language. He was going to make this idea work no matter what it took.

No matter how many stupid details he had to wade through.

"It's time we had a talk about my idea," Paul said as he leaned against the bar and shoved thoughts of Libby aside.

The thoughts would be back, he knew it. But he had to try.

Des watched him from the corner of his eye as he scribbled a note onto the staff roster. "Is that so?"

"Yep." He nodded. "I'm ready to take it seriously."

"Good." Curiosity colored his brother's expression. "What caused that?"

Paul reached for the printed plans he'd stashed in a folder behind the bar and handed one to his brother. "I realized that I needed something more in my life than what I have now, and I need to fight for it. I thought I was sick of trying to prove myself, but I realized it wasn't about that. It's about giving myself my best shot at success."

Des nodded, his eyes scanning the front page of the plan.

"I still want to start up my own mixology school. Since we now officially have Libby's vodkas here, I want to keep that partnership." He tried to keep his face neutral but even saying her name was like stabbing himself in the chest. "If you look at page three—"

"That's a brilliant idea." Des looked up from the report.

"You haven't even read the whole plan."

"Paul…" Des laid a hand on his shoulder. "I never questioned the idea when you brought it to me before, but I wanted to know you were invested in it. I take my business seriously, and I want my partners to do the same."

He hadn't thought that hearing his brother say that would be so relieving… His family was everything to him. "There's no one else I'd rather do business with." Des stuck out his hand, and Paul shook it firmly. "Let me look over the report at home, and we can talk through the plans in more detail. I'll want to make sure the numbers are sound, but I like the idea. I think you'll be brilliant."

"Great, because we have a group coming through this week to try it out." Paul grinned. It was a risk, but he knew the idea was solid. He'd show Des that he wasn't the only Chapman with an entrepreneurial mind.

Des rolled his eyes. "What if I'd thought it was a terrible idea?"

"Then I would have done it anyway to prove you wrong."

His brother clapped him on the back. "You sticking around tonight?"

"Nah," he said, wiping down the bar and stacking the remaining glasses into the dishwasher.

"Still avoiding Libby, I see." Des shook his head.

"Tonight is her night, I don't want to spoil it." He swallowed down the pain that reared up whenever he thought of her.

Against his will, he missed her like crazy. If he managed to go a day without consciously thinking about her then his dreams would be filled with her sweet face. Memories, fantasies, and wishes all combining to torture him night after night.

"Do you really believe you'd spoil it by being here to support her?" His brother sighed. "Don't you think that's *exactly* what she wants?"

"You know the whole engagement and everything was fake. We weren't really in…" He couldn't force himself to say the *L* word.

"Weren't you? You're not as good an actor as you seem to think you are."

"I fooled you, didn't I? And everyone else." He turned away so his brother wouldn't see the struggle going on inside him.

"I think you're trying to fool yourself, and you're failing," Des said. "If that relationship was a scam then why were you happier when she was around?"

Paul slammed the dishwasher door shut and jabbed a finger at the start button. "Who says I was happier?"

"My dishwasher, for one."

Paul turned and folded his arms across his chest. "Any other inanimate objects able to back that up? Does the blender want to weigh in, too?"

Des shook his head. "You're so full of shit sometimes. The way you looked at that girl wasn't a scam, it wasn't fake, and it certainly wasn't you being a good actor. I look at Gracie the same way, I *know* what it means."

"It doesn't matter anyway. We're not together now, and that's not going to change." He didn't add that there wasn't a hope in hell of Libby taking him back even if he did go groveling back to her.

Which he couldn't…could he?

No…he'd been momentarily fooled into thinking relationships could work. Nothing more.

Des motioned for one of his staff to start unpacking the boxes of decorations that had arrived earlier that afternoon. "I've never seen you look at a woman that way before. Not even Sadie."

Paul folded his arms across his chest. "It was all part of the act."

The words rang hollow in his ears. Meaningless.

It wasn't an act, and hadn't he decided to give up lying to his family after the wedding?

"If you say so." Des shrugged in a way that confirmed the words sounded as believable as they felt.

"She wouldn't take me back anyway." But he wanted her to, despite the fact that his conversation with Sadie had cemented the concerns that already existed. And if the pain he felt now was anything to go by, losing Libby after being with her for a longer period of time could prove fatal.

He sighed. He was miserable without her, that couldn't be denied…but love?

Yes. It was true, he'd never looked at another girl the way he looked at her. He'd never *felt* about another girl the way he felt about her.

"You don't know that." Des pulled a bottle of tequila

down from the spirits shelf and poured two shots.

"What are the shots for?" Paul asked warily.

"Dutch courage." Des slid one glass over to him and picked up the other in his right hand. "*Salute!*"

They clinked glasses and downed the shots. The tequila warmed his insides, filling him with a comfortable glow. He'd need more than a shot's worth of courage to lay himself at Libby's mercy. He wasn't sure there were enough shots in all the world.

But that was the point, wasn't it? Big risk for big reward.

"You're an idiot if you don't think she's worth dealing with a little fear."

He couldn't deny it, a lie of that magnitude could not pass his lips. "I don't know if I can."

"So you gave the ring back to Ma?"

The ring was in his wallet as it had been since Libby had left it on the table next to the bed the night of the wedding. He'd carried it around for a month, telling himself that he was going to give it back to his mother. Instead, he'd kept it close to him every day while he thought about how much he'd fucked things up with Libby.

"I'll take that brooding silence as no," Des said smugly.

"What would you be doing now if you'd never been with Sadie?"

Paul looked up. "What do you mean?"

"If you'd never been cheated on, would you still be avoiding the situation with Libby?"

"I don't know. How can I answer that?" He sighed. "It's not like I can pretend it never happened."

Des nodded. "Sure, but you don't have to use it as a yardstick for life."

It was a crazy thought. How *would* he act if he'd never gone through that situation? If he'd never been brought to his knees by someone he cared about?

Possibilities swirled in his mind. Some good, some terrifying. But the possibility that history wouldn't repeat itself had taken root in his mind, warming him like she had done so many times before. Tempting him with what could be.

Tonight was her night. He wasn't going to steal her thunder by throwing his issues onto her shoulders. He loved her…and for the moment that meant letting her bask in the glow of her success.

"Regardless, I can't stay. Libby will have plenty of people here who care about her, I'm not going to distract her on her big night."

Des threw his hands up in the air. "Then you're in the same category as her father."

"What's that supposed to mean?"

"She's been trying to get him to come along tonight, but the bastard won't return her calls. We had a few drinks when she came in to finalize the fit out for tonight, and she told me he's avoiding her." He raked a hand through his hair. "So *I* called him. Told him I was Libby's PR manager."

"And?" Paul didn't like where this was going.

"He said he had better things to do with his time than watch his daughter throw her life down the drain."

"Did she hear him say that?"

He shook his head. "No, she doesn't know I called him. She used my phone one night to see if he'd take her call if he didn't recognize the number but he didn't answer…so I called him on my own."

Kirk Harris was in a league of his own when it came

to being a bastard. Libby deserved so much more from her family…and she deserved so much more from him. It might be too late, but he loved her, dammit. And now he had an idea of how he might be able to make it up to her.

"You're not coming?" Libby felt as though her stomach had fallen through the floor. "Why?"

"John has to work late, and I can't find anyone to babysit Eloise. She's not old enough to stay home on her own yet." Her mother's wariness radiated down the phone line. "I'm sorry, Libby. That's part of being a mother."

Libby bit back a retort about the fact that she was also *her* mother, not just Eloise's. But being jealous of a ten-year-old was a lesson in futility, as was trying to get her parents to put her first for a change.

"You could always bring her along."

"To a bar?" Her mother sighed. "That's not appropriate."

Libby was officially two for two. Her mother had canceled on her at the last minute, and she hadn't even been able to get in touch with her father. No amount of voicemails had yielded a return phone call, and all her texts had gone unanswered. She'd even swung past his house, but the sight of wife number four had made her turn tail.

There would be zero family at the launch of Libby Gal Cocktails.

After saying a few words to Eloise, who was adamant about relaying her whole school day to Libby in minute detail, she hung up the phone. The girl had it so good, and she didn't even know.

"No dice?" Nina asked.

She was barefoot, her bright blue hair—which was now showing a line of blond at the roots—twisted into a knot. A stack of professionally printed posters featuring Nina's artwork sat on the coffee table, the watercolor designs a melange of pink, green, and yellow. Tonight those posters would decorate the walls of First and from tomorrow onward they'd feature on her website and the advertising she'd booked with local magazines and blogs.

She was finally launching her business...without her family, without Paul. If it weren't for Nina's ever-supportive presence she'd be truly alone in the world.

"She couldn't get a babysitter for Eloise." Libby turned to her computer so she wouldn't see Nina's sympathy.

But Nina wasn't the kind of person who would let her get away with it that easily. "That's really shitty."

Libby swallowed, nodding. Praying she wouldn't cry and mess up the artful makeup application she'd treated herself to...and paid a small fortune for.

"Have you heard from Paul?" Nina sat on the edge of her desk, one leg crossed over the other.

As much as Nina abhorred pink, she'd worn a pair of fuchsia jeans to go with the pink and green gingham shirts they'd had made for the wait staff for tonight's event. She *never* wore pink, but she hadn't complained once.

"Are you trying to pour salt on the wound?" Libby shook her head. "No, I haven't heard from him."

"Have you called him?"

"Why would I call him, Neens? He made it clear we weren't an item, and now his whole family knows the relationship was a sham." She reached for a bottle of her lavender vodka and two shot glasses. "I have nothing to say to him."

"Not all relationships are destined to fail, you know."

Libby's head snapped up. She'd expected a snappy comeback from her best friend, a declaration that Paul was indeed a Grade A jerk or, at the very least, that Libby didn't need a man to make her happy. Which was true, she didn't... but Paul *had* made her happy, and she couldn't seem to forget it.

"You know Pete and I split up once," Nina continued. "Before we got engaged."

"I didn't know that." Libby twisted the lid off the vodka and inhaled the relaxing lavender scent.

"He wanted to go overseas for six months, and I couldn't leave my job for that long. I told him I didn't want to hold him back, that I didn't want to change him. So he went." Nina's hand came down on Libby's, her sparkly black nail polish glimmering in the afternoon light. "I was so fucking miserable without him, you have no idea. He came back within a week and told me it was the stupidest thing he'd ever done."

"Smart man."

"What I'm saying is, sometimes you need to experience that separation to know how much you care about someone. You need to understand what life is like without him." She grinned. "Besides, boys are stupid. We can't crucify them for every little mistake."

"What if Pete hadn't come back?"

"I'd already booked a flight to Tuscany to be with him." She patted Libby's hand. "Being apart didn't feel right to either of us."

"I don't know what being apart feels like for him." She poured the vodka into two shot glasses, her hand shaking, and she spilled a little onto her desk.

"That's because you haven't asked him."

"But I *did*. He told me there was nothing between us." Libby took a long breath. "He's right, I'm not…relationship material. I'm not family material, either."

"Don't you ever say that!" Nina jumped off the desk and wrapped her arms around Libby. "Family isn't just the people you're related to, you idiot. It's the people you choose to be part of your life. You're my family, and I'll shout it from the rooftops if I have to."

"Really?" Libby's eyes swam.

"I'll even get a bullshit Facebook account and put it on the internet if that helps you believe it."

Libby laughed through the haze of tears. "Wow, wearing pink and succumbing to Facebook. You must love me."

"Damn straight, and don't you forget it."

Libby placed one of the filled vodka shots in front of Nina. "Bottoms up."

It was Nina's turn to look serious. "No can do, my little flower."

"I thought you said heavy drinking is recommended in times of intense stress." Libby picked up her glass and downed the drink.

"Yeah, but it's not recommended for pregnant ladies."

Libby's mouth fell open. "You're pregnant?"

"I'm only eight weeks along, so don't you *dare* tell anybody." She fiddled with the large hoop in her ear. "But, seeing as there's all this talk about family…I wanted to make it official. I want you to be my baby's godmother."

Libby's heart beat like a drum, pounding her ribcage and flooding her body with all the love she'd locked up safe and tight. All the love she'd held inside for fear of giving it to someone and having him throw it away.

"I would be honored," she said, squeezing her friend. "I'm going to be the best godmother there ever was."

"I have no doubt. And I mean what I said, you *are* part of my family." Nina patted her belly and smiled. "You're part of my baby's family. I need someone he or she can look up to, because Pete and I sure as hell aren't great role models."

Libby pulled a face. "You're going to be an amazing mother."

"So are you one day. A great wife, a great mother, a great grandmother. If you pull your head out of your ass, that is." Nina patted her shoulder.

For the first time the idea of being any or all of those things didn't fill her with fear and scepticism. She had an opportunity to fill someone else's life with love and happiness, to do the opposite of what her parents had done.

And Paul...the time apart hadn't diminished her feelings for him. Not by a long shot.

"Tonight you need to concentrate on being a great businesswoman." Nina jumped up and brushed her hands down her thighs. "But call that stupid boy tomorrow, and show him what he's missing."

She had no idea if he missed her, if he regretted what he'd said...if the words were even true. And she wanted to be in Nina's shoes, to have a family of her own. To grow old with someone, to be a good influence and share her success with someone. But there wasn't anyone else she could imagine spending her life with other than Paul.

Outside First, the late afternoon sun waned. Summer had given way to autumn, and with it came intermittent drizzle—a much needed reprieve from the heat—and shorter days. Gray clouds hovered overhead, a warning to stay indoors.

Paul stalked toward his car, a dark cloud of his own crushing down on him. Des's comment had struck him deep in the chest, in that soft place only a loved one could find. His brother certainly counted as a loved one, but right now he wanted to punch him in the face.

Paul was *not* in the same category as Kirk Harris.

He got into his car and slammed the door shut behind him. Poor Libby. She must be devastated that her father wasn't coming along tonight.

Drumming his fingers on the steering wheel, he finally let memories of Libby wash over him. He pictured her face so clearly she could have been standing in front of him—her sharp hazel eyes, that sweet smile, and her mane of coin-colored hair.

Des was right about one thing: Paul *had* been happy when she was in his life.

Since the wedding there'd been a great big hole in his life, a joy-sucking void that made him miserable. He'd thrown himself into planning for the mixology school, but even that hadn't satisfied him the way it should. Family dinners had been missed, phone calls ignored. He only left the house to work at First and even then he had to drag himself there.

The solution was painfully clear. He wanted Libby in his

life. He missed her with a soul-aching sadness so deep and dark it stole his slumber night after night. He missed her smile, her laugh, the way she lifted him up. Made him better.

And he couldn't ignore it, the past month had taught him that much.

He loved her. He never wanted to, never hoped to...but he did.

If anyone was throwing anything down the drain it wasn't Libby and her career, it was him. Letting fear and stupidity rule his actions. No more. She was worth the risk. Undoubtedly.

All he had to do now was hope that she'd forgive him.

As he started up his car and pulled out into the busy South Melbourne traffic, a plan began coming together in his mind.

Chapter Seventeen

Libby's hand trembled as she put her hand on the door to First. In less than an hour the room would be filled with local media, bloggers, business owners, and friends all in attendance to celebrate the official launch of her business.

Inside the restaurant was a flurry of activity. Pink and green paper lanterns had been strung from the ceiling along with strands of fairy lights, giving the room the garden party vibe she'd wanted. Fresh flowers dotted the high standing tables that had replaced the regular furniture and the waiters wore green and pink checkered shirts.

Smoothing her hands down the front of her fuchsia dress, she sucked in a breath. Everything was in its place, the room was exactly as she wanted it…but something was missing.

A tiny part of her had hoped that Paul would be here. Even if there was no hope of them being together, knowing she had his support would have meant something. But he was nowhere to be seen.

Des stood behind the bar in his usual black T-shirt, directing the staff on how to set up the visual merchandising. Noah carried boxes back and forth, unpacking the last of the promotional goodies.

"Are you excited?" Nina asked, walking up to her after dispensing the artwork to one of Des's staff members.

"I'm excited to see you wearing that outfit." Libby laughed, pushing away the hollow feeling in her chest. Tonight was a special night, and she wouldn't let stupid things like emotions ruin it for her.

"Anything for you." Nina shook her head. "I don't know how you wear pink. I feel like a fucking cupcake."

"And you look just as delicious," Libby teased.

Her eyes continued to scan the room. Apparently her heart was not yet ready to give up on the idea that he might show.

"He's not here." Des put a reassuring hand on her shoulder. "He left about twenty minutes ago."

"Oh." A lump lodged in Libby's throat. At least she had her answer. Now she could move on and throw all her energy back into her business. "His loss, I guess."

"Couldn't agree more."

Guests filtered into the room. Libby recognized a columnist from *Gastronomy* magazine as well as a popular lifestyle and fashion blogger. Her heart jackhammered in her chest.

She kept herself busy as she fussed over the displays. The cocktails that had been designed for the event—Paul's handiwork, she suspected, though Des would not confirm—sat in pretty rows along the bar.

"These look fantastic," she said, peering at a set of martini glasses that had been dusted with super-fine sugar crystals and decorated with sprigs of fresh lavender.

"The lavender martini should be a hit. We've put it on the specials board this week, and it's doing really well." He grinned, his newly tanned skin making his smile appear even brighter. "We're going to do good business together."

"Thank you for everything." She looked up at him. "After what I did you should have turned me out."

"You wouldn't have needed to go to such lengths if I'd seen the potential from the start. I appreciate you both coming clean, though." His dark eyes reminded her so much of Paul that she had to turn away.

"You deserved that much at least."

"And you deserve everything, too, Libby. Don't ever forget that." He turned her around to face the room.

The crowd had swelled, and the waiters had begun distributing trays of food matched to the first cocktail on circulation. All cocktails had been served in smaller glasses to allow people to taste multiple drinks. Miniature pink Bellinis made their way around, and people drank, smiling and talking among themselves.

"You'd better mingle," Des said. "I'm sure there'll be plenty of questions for you."

"You're right." Libby grabbed a mini Bellini for herself and made her way to a group of very fashionable-looking young women whom she suspected were from a bridal magazine she'd contacted.

"Go get 'em!" Des called out after her.

B y the time Paul had made it to his destination, Libby's party had already started. He'd be late.

Better late than never, right?

He leaned against the car, staring up at the two-story town house in South Yarra that Libby had grown up in. The white building contrasted sharply to the ornate black fretwork lining the balcony and the black trim on the huge bay windows on each floor.

The lawn looked as though it had never seen a harsh summer, the plants gleaming vibrant green in the faded early evening light. It was perfect. Pristine. Expensive. Not a blade of grass out of place.

Kirk Harris was home. Paul had gotten ahold of his secretary to confirm it, though getting the address wasn't as easy. He'd charmed the woman into believing he had a delivery for the current Mrs. Harris that would put Mr. Harris in a vulnerable position should it not be delivered.

Feigning an incorrect delivery address, Paul had wheedled his way into the street name, and he already knew what car the man drove. Bentleys were more common in South Yarra than in other suburbs, but not *that* common.

Now all he had to do was work up the courage to knock on the door.

He wasn't thrilled about facing Libby's father again… not after their last encounter. But it had to be done if he was going to marry her. The thought washed him with a deep calm.

Libby would want her father there tonight. Why else would she have called him repeatedly to invite him? Deep down he knew there was a chance the plan could backfire horribly. But the risk would be worth it.

He walked up the path and knocked on the door before his resolve escaped him. A moment later Kirk answered the door himself.

"Yes?" he asked, taking a moment to register Paul's identity. "What the hell do *you* want?"

"I was hoping I could have a minute of your time, Dr. Harris."

The older man laughed, folding his arms across his chest. "So I'm *Dr. Harris* now. There's a change."

"I know we didn't exactly get started in the best way—"

"No, you threatened me and kicked me out of my own property. I'd say that's a very poor impression to leave on the father of your girlfriend."

"I know. But I can't apologize for that. You were treating Libby unfairly, and I had to stick up for her." He hoped the gamble of his honesty would pay off.

Kirk Harris might be a lot of things, but he didn't appear to be stupid. Insincerity would be a red flag. Paul was better off showing his cards and hoping he respected him for that.

"Then why are you here if not to apologize?"

"I have a favor to ask."

Silence. Hazel eyes—Libby's eyes—regarded him without giving anything away, as Kirk leaned against the doorframe. He hadn't told Paul to get lost, so that had to count for something.

"You're starting with a low bargaining position," Kirk warned.

"It's not a favor for me…it's for Libby."

"Ah. She gets you to do her dirty work, does she? Her mother was like that."

Paul bit back the urge to retort, instead jamming his

hands into his pockets to keep himself from punching Kirk. "She doesn't know I'm here. But she has an important event tonight. It's the launch of her business. She wants you to be there."

"I already told that PR boy of hers I'm not interested. When my daughter comes back to doing what she should be doing, then I'll attend anything she likes."

"Right." Paul nodded. "So it's conditional then."

"What is?"

"Your love." He paused for a moment to watch Kirk's brow crease. "That's good to know. I bet Libby has suspected it, but hearing that confirmed will be good for her. Not now, but in the long run."

"Criticize me when you have children of your own. It's not as easy as you think."

"I will. But I can tell you now, if I'm lucky enough to have a child with Libby there's no way in hell I'll ever hold him or her over a barrel to get what I want." He forced himself to breathe, to talk slowly. Deliberately. "I disagree with my parents all the time. But I know, no matter whether or not we can settle an argument, they love me. I've never doubted it. Libby does."

Kirk had the decency to look shocked. "I've given her *everything,* how could she think I don't love her?"

"Because you won't even support her on the biggest night of her life. She's making something of herself, and you're ignoring her calls because you're too selfish to put her dreams before your own."

For a moment Paul was certain Kirk would turn him away. His lips pressed together into a flat line, his jaw locked. Tight. A vein pulsed in his forehead, breaking the frosty exterior he'd presented so far.

"I want her to go back to finish her studies."

"She might, but she might not. If she doesn't, are you prepared to cut all ties with her? Are you prepared to miss out on birthdays and Christmases and weddings because she refused to go back to school?" Paul shook his head. "You can't keep hurting her. All she wants is for you to support her, to say you care about what *she* wants."

"What she wants is wrong." The words sounded tough, but a crack had appeared.

Paul looked past Kirk into the fancy house. Polish boards lined the floor, and a crystal chandelier hung in the entrance along with a gilt mirror and some expensive-looking art. All this money, this fortunate life, and Kirk still wasn't happy with what he had.

It was sad.

"I'm going to ask Libby to marry me," Paul said, speaking the words as slowly and calmly as his racing mind would allow. "Tonight."

His heart pounded. The decision hadn't been made until the moment the words were out of his mouth, but nothing else in his life had ever felt so right.

"Is this you asking my permission?"

"I don't need your permission and, as much as I would like your blessing, that isn't necessary, either." He pulled his shoulders back, preparing to walk away without achieving his goal. "But I promise you that I'll take care of her the best I can. I'll support her dreams, I'll keep her safe, and I'll make sure she feels loved every single day. I'll give her what she's missing."

Kirk sighed. "You know, I don't doubt that at all."

He saw some of Libby in her father then, in the way his hazel eyes focused in while he analyzed the situation. They were both ambitious, tough. Fighters.

"I turned up at Libby's grandparents' doorstep once, too." Kirk nodded, his eyes locked onto something in the distance. "I tried to convince them to let Libby's mother back into their home after she got pregnant. I failed."

"Come along tonight, tell Libby you're happy for her. She doesn't need much, you being there will be enough."

Baby steps. Kirk might not back down on trying to convince Libby to go back to school, but they didn't have to agree on everything. Maybe if he could see all she'd achieved he would understand.

"Fine." Kirk grabbed his keys and phone from a table in the entrance and followed Paul down to where their cars were parked on the street.

The launch party had turned out even better than Libby could have imagined. She'd already been interviewed by a columnist for a major newspaper—not something she was expecting—and the blogging crowd had taken a real shine to her.

She'd posed for photos and answered questions about everything from her business model to her thoughts on cocktail and flavor trends. She'd taken selfies, swapped business cards, and had even met with one of the restaurant managers who'd turned her down initially. Turns out locally sourced, small batch product *was* appealing to restaurant clientele over tacky celebrity endorsement.

Still, she couldn't deny how much sweeter victory would taste if she had Paul by her side. Smoothing her hands down the front of her dress, she turned to make conversation with the man next to her, but the words died on her lips when his face registered.

"Dad?"

Her father smiled but didn't reach out to embrace her or touch her in any way. That wasn't his style. "Libby. Congratulations on your launch."

"Thank you." She swallowed, fighting back the excitement that bubbled in her chest like fizzing champagne. "I wasn't expecting you."

"No, I guess you weren't." He cleared his throat. "I would like to say…"

"Yes?"

"I'm proud of you." The words sounded as stiff as over-starched shirts, but gushing praise would never happen. This was as much as she would get from him.

She touched his arm, desperate for some physical connection. "You are?"

He nodded. "I know I can be…difficult sometimes. But I care about you."

"I appreciate that, Dad."

"And I still think you should go back to school."

Her stomach dropped. Had he really come all this way to push his own agenda? She tugged on the skirt of her dress, distracting herself from arguing with him.

"But," he continued with a sigh, "I know I could be more supportive with what you want to do. I do want what's best for you, even if we don't agree on what that is."

His words were a balm to her soul. "I love you, Dad."

"I love you, too, Libby. Now, I suppose I should try one of these drinks." He looked around, not smiling but not judging, either.

"Let me grab one for you." She flagged down a waiter and picked up a Caipiroska made with her lemon myrtle vodka. "Try this."

"I'm sorry I called it toxic cordial." He said, taking a sip.

"I know you didn't mean it." She hadn't really, but he being here now was the proof she needed to keep trying at this relationship. "I'm curious, how did you end up getting the details for tonight? I never sent you the invitation in the end."

"Someone paid me a visit." The barest hint of a smile crossed his lips. "Seems that boyfriend of yours *is* good for something."

Paul had ushered Kirk through the front door and then slipped into First via the staff entrance out in the alley. He wanted Libby to have a chance to talk with her father, and he didn't want to risk her seeing him until he was absolutely prepared. Though judging by the way his whole body felt like it was suffering through an earthquake, feeling prepared was a luxury he would not experience tonight.

He spotted her immediately. Through the throngs of fashionable people all dressed up and enjoying themselves, she shined like a lone star. Envy twinged in his gut as she charmed two men, making them laugh and shake their heads as she talked animatedly.

He couldn't have been prouder than if he were right

there by her side.

"Paolo?"

Hearing his name caught him off guard and he turned to see his mother, watching him closely.

"Ma, what are you doing here?"

"I'm here for Libby," she said, folding her arms across her chest in a way that spoke far louder than her actual words. "I thought you weren't coming."

"I had a change of heart."

"I'm glad to see you have some sense left in your head." Her dark eyes narrowed at him. "To think you were going to leave that poor girl all alone…"

"You know that we broke up." He shook his head.

"Yes, and I know you told everyone that you weren't really engaged, but I noticed that you haven't bothered to return the ring to me." The smug smile tugging at her lips made him laugh. "I know why."

"Oh do you now?"

"You're in love with her, and you're not pretending this time."

Busted. His mother really should have been a gossip reporter. "You're guessing."

"I'm not. I know you better than anyone," she said. "You made me very sad, you know."

Great, here comes the guilt trip.

"For breaking up with her?"

She shook her head as though he'd disappointed her. "For thinking you needed to lie to me. Do I want you to get married? Yes. Do I want you to have babies? Yes. But I love you no matter what."

"Even if I stayed a bachelor my whole life?"

"Even then." She wrinkled her nose. "Don't get any ideas, though."

"I won't."

Her eyes twinkled. "Promise?"

"Cross my heart."

"I love you, Paolo. I want you to be happy, and I will support you no matter what." She sighed. "I want to support Libby, too, she's a good girl. A *smart* girl."

"You think she's too good for me?" he teased.

His mother shook her head solemnly. "I think she's perfect for you."

He swallowed against the lump in his throat. "Me, too."

"You'd better make it right."

"I know." His eyes returned to the goddess with the red hair. "I've taken stupid to a new level."

"She deserves more than a fake engagement." There was no malice in her voice. "You need to give her anything she asks for."

"No, I'll give her *everything*." The edges of the ring bit into his palm where he held it tight.

He slipped behind the bar and did what he knew best. He assembled the cocktail he'd planned on the drive over, combining the orange juice, champagne, and Libby's basil and orange vodka into a champagne flute. He cut the peel from an orange so that it curled, just the way he'd done the first night she came into the bar. Then he threaded the ring onto a cocktail stick and secured it, with the orange, over the edge of the glass.

She hadn't yet noticed him as she flitted from guest to guest. She spoke to a group of young women who typed notes into their phones as she answered questions, and then they took photos with her and the drinks.

Then he saw her talking with Kirk. He waited for yelling, for tears, or for one of them storming off. But when she handed her father a drink, he caught a smile on her lips. Relief. Happiness.

Paul waited until she took a moment to breathe, then he left the cocktail on the bar and went to find her. The crowd was entertained, and Paul could tell from the arrival of the marshmallow rose martinis that they were onto the second to last course. He walked up behind her, taking a moment to admire the curl of her hair down her back, the copper tones shining against her pink dress.

"How does it feel to be the lady of the hour?"

She spun around, her eyes wide. The color in her cheeks bloomed, and she blinked. "It would feel better if I weren't on my own."

"That's a far cry from the girl who said I wasn't allowed to fall in love with her." He reached for her hand but she stepped backward.

"Looks like my warning worked a little too well, I think." She pursed her lips. They were the exact shade of pink as her dress.

"Can we talk?"

"The last time I asked you that you looked as though I wanted to give you a lobotomy."

"Perhaps you should have," he said drily. "My head needed fixing."

A ghost of a smile passed over her lips. "I'm in the middle of the biggest night of my life."

"Tiger, this is only the beginning. You're never going to stop lighting up the room."

She sipped her drink and looked away from him. "I told you not to call me Tiger."

"And then you started liking it."

She shook her head, but her cheeks flushed even deeper. "I heard you brought a plus one with you."

"Or perhaps I was the plus one."

Her features softened. "You were always invited. I wanted you to be here."

"Five minutes, that's all I want." He took her hand, and this time she allowed him.

He led her behind the bar. Amongst the other cocktails she didn't notice the one he'd prepared specially for her.

"Tick tock." She tapped her wrist. "I'm working tonight."

"How can I say this succinctly? I've been an asshole."

A smile twitched at the corner of her lips. "So we're in agreement then."

"I lied to you. When you asked me if our relationship was fake, I lied." He drew a deep breath.

"Why?" She fiddled with her necklace, her fingers running over the pendant swinging on the end of a fine chain. "You made me feel like I was nothing."

"The thought of losing you was…excruciating."

"But you *did* lose me—you pushed me away." Her voice shook.

"I thought it would be easier to deal with the pain now than face it every day." He clenched his jaw, the words sticking in his throat. "I knew you would leave eventually."

"Why did you think that?"

He didn't answer, but the look on her face told him she understood.

"I'm not her, Paul. She wanted something else, something

fictional." She sighed. "You can't blame yourself for that and, more importantly, you can't paint me with the same brush."

"I know. You…" He looked her in the eye. "You inspire me, Libby. Every bit of my speech was about you, about how you made me feel. I was terrified."

"I terrified you?" She raised a brow.

"You made me feel like I wanted to try again. Like it would be worth the risk to put myself out there." He stepped closer to her. "I haven't felt that in a long time."

"Me, either," she whispered. "But you can't back down because you're scared."

"I'm not scared anymore." He touched her cheek, and she closed her eyes.

"That's not enough."

"How about this? I love you, Libby Harris." He forced her face to tilt up to his. "Look at me. I love you with all my heart. I could not be more proud of you tonight, of everything you've achieved. You make me want to be a better person, and I promise you I will work every day to be the man you deserve."

"I want you to be the man *you* want to be, not what you think is best for me."

"That's just it, I was what I thought I wanted to be until you came along. I didn't think there was anything else I had to give, but you changed that."

Her eyes softened. "Really?"

"Yes, really."

"If it means anything, I never wanted to fall in love with you," she said with a cheeky smile. She touched her hand to his chest and pulled him closer.

"I'm not sure how that is supposed to make me feel

better."

"What I mean is, nothing could have stopped me falling in love with you. Not logic, not reason, not my stupid ideas about what love means."

"Nor mine."

She smiled. "I don't want you to push me away or clam up when things get tough. *That's* how we're going to stay together."

"I promise." He nodded, a calm washing over him and soothing the pains of the past. "We should celebrate."

"To love?" she asked.

He reached over to the bar and handed her the cocktail. "To marriage."

The ring caught the light, and her mouth dropped open.

"I don't think I've ever seen you speechless before." He held the ring carefully and unthreaded it from the cocktail stick. "Hold out your hand, I want to do this properly."

Her hand shaking, she clasped the drink in her right hand and held out her left. He slipped the ring onto her finger, twirling it so that it shone in the light.

"Libby Harris, will you marry me?" He held her hand. "For real this time."

"Yes," she said, her eyes shining. "On one condition."

"What's that?"

"Don't ever stop calling me Tiger."

"Anything for you."

"I guess this means I can stop looking for a new place to live." She smiled, pressing her cheek against his chest.

The crowd erupted in a raucous cheer as he brought his mouth down to hers and kissed her deeply, but in that moment it was like they were the only two people in all the world. The orange and champagne danced on his tongue as he tasted her, clasping her hand in his, relishing the feel of the ring on her finger.

"There's half a bed with your name on it, Tiger, and I can't wait to wake up beside you."

"I'm all yours." She grinned and wrapped her hands around his neck, dragging his lips back to hers. "Forever and ever."

Acknowledgments

I would not be where I am today without the love and support of my husband. He has backed me from day one and is always the first person to tell me I can do something, no matter how big and scary the task may be.

Thank you to Mum, Dad, Sami, and Albie for always checking in on me and for making me feel loved even if we are in different hemispheres.

To all the readers who've taken the time to leave a star rating, a review, or to send me a comment or email, thank you. Knowing that people enjoy my books brings me an immense amount of joy, and your support means the world to me. Happy reading!

About the Author

Originally from Melbourne, Stefanie now lives in Toronto with her wonderful husband. She loves to read, collect lipsticks, watch zombie movies, and drink coffee. By day (and night!) she writes contemporary romance with humor, heat, and heart, and tries not to spend too much time shopping online and watching baby animal videos on YouTube.

To find out more about her upcoming releases be sure to sign up for her newsletter: http://eepurl.com/bbhIsD

Also by Stefanie London...

THE RULES ACCORDING TO GRACIE

Gracie Green has a shopping list for men. Career, financials, family...and a long list of rules to determine a guy's suitability. Too bad she keeps getting distracted by her super-sexy, six-feet-of-tattooed-hotness friend, Des Chapman, who is *so* many shades of Mr. Wrong. As Gracie's discouragement grows, Des realizes it's time to show Gracie what she really needs in a man. He'll teach Gracie the Rules According To Des—even if it means breaking *his* one rule in the process.